FIGHT FOR IT

AMY L. GALE

USA TODAY BESTSELLING AUTHOR
AMY L. GALE

Fight For It © 2021 Amy L Gale

Copyright notice: All rights reserved under the International and Pan-American Copyright Conventions. No part of this book may be reproduced or transmitted in any form or by any means, electronic or mechanical, including photocopying, recording, or by any information storage and retrieval system, without permission in writing from the publisher.

This is a work of fiction. Names, places, characters and incidents are either the product of the author's imagination or are used fictitiously, and any resemblance to any actual persons, living or dead, organizations, events or locales is entirely coincidental.

Warning: the unauthorized reproduction or distribution of this copyrighted work is illegal. Criminal copyright infringement, including infringement without monetary gain, is investigated by the FBI and is punishable by up to 5 years in prison and a fine of $250,000.

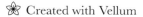 Created with Vellum

1

BEWARE THE KRAKEN

"Come on, punch me in the face." Mason, a teenager from down the street who clearly has no clue how to interact with the human race, says while standing in front of our hometown hero. "You know, for pretend while I snap a selfie."

Sure, having Ray "The Wrecker" Wilson back here in Sunset Cove is the talk of the town, but everyone doesn't need to lose their minds. I haven't had people line up outside my real estate office…well, ever. I guess it's kind of cool. A boxing legend returning to Sunset Cove. Other than Ray, our celebrity status stops at the local news anchors.

Ray puts his fist up to Mason's chin and they both smile. Flashes of light fill the room. Am I at a Hollywood premiere? I didn't even know there were this many reporters in our small beach town. Might as well enjoy my fifteen minutes of fame.

I pat down my navy blazer and toss my hair over a shoulder as Ray approaches. Glad I had time for a dye job and some highlights. I'm guessing the photo ops will be endless.

My mind races back to high school. Ray and my brother Rick were joined at the hip. I take a deep breath and flash a million dollar smile. Why the hell am I so nervous? It's not like he'll remember I'm Rick's kid sister. I've come a long way from those days, just like him.

Ray walks towards me. I breathe slowly, trying to control my heartrate which tripled in the last five seconds. He runs a hand through his thick brown hair and I'm transported back to Filmore High. Every time Ray walked into a room, he ran those fingers through his hair. It's like it was his trademark. I guess it still holds true. My brother Rick used to call the move the "panty dropper". Girls flocked to Ray like moths flying toward a light, unable to stop themselves. Jesus, does it have the same effect on me?

"Ray Wilson, we spoke on the phone." He holds out his hand.

I lift my hand to meet his, trying to stop it from trembling.

He squints and tips his chin to the side. "Lys Adams?"

I flash a smile and nod. "Alyssa Higgins...well, for now."

He lunges forward and pulls me into a bear hug, just about sweeping me off of my feet. "I'd know those green eyes anywhere." He releases me and takes a step back. "Look at you, you're gorgeous."

I let out a chuckle like a school girl back in the 50's who's just been asked to the prom by the captain of the football team. It's been a long time since anyone has complemented me on my looks. "It's great to see you to Ray." It's not like I could tell him I had a major crush on him for my whole high school career. It doesn't matter anyway. I'm here to help him buy the Kraken Bar and Grill, not flirt.

He turns back toward the reporters for a second and then slings an arm around my shoulder. "Get one of me and Lys for the paper. She's setting me up with the Kraken and it's going to be better than ever."

Tingles sweep from my head to my toes the second he touches me. My body temperature skyrockets to about a thousand degrees. I flash the best smile I can and take a step back. "Okay, do you guys have everything you need?" I say to the reporters flashing lights at me like I'm at a 90's nightclub. If I don't get some space between Ray and I, there's a good chance I'll burst into flames.

"Yes, Ms. Higgins. We're all set. Ray, good luck with your new business, and it's great to have you back." The head reporter tips his hat at Ray.

"Best place in the world to be." Ray waves. He turns toward me.

Oh right, the paperwork. "I have about a hundred papers for you to sign to make this official." I search his face. Perfect jawline, blue eyes that can pierce an armored truck, and skin so smooth any girl would kill for it. No wonder everyone always said he's way too pretty to be a boxer. He's like a white tiger, astonishing to look at but deadly if the situation requires.

That sexy smile hasn't left his face since he walked into the room. "Sounds like it'll take forever. How about some lunch while I sign my life away?" Ray gestures toward the door.

Okay, Ray's super sweet. Always has been, but I need to keep this professional. Besides, news spreads through Sunset Cove like wildfire. My recent ex-husband Jared would have two birds and a chicken if he heard that I was at lunch with

Ray. Since he and his brother run the town, I have to watch myself since Jared's wounds from the divorce are still fresh.

I open my mouth to speak but Ray beats me to it. "Come on, Lys. Let's hit Johnny's Diner." He nudges me with his elbow. "Remember the time you dumped your chocolate milkshake on Connie D'amico?"

Oh God, I completely forgot about it. Connie was dating my brother and cheated on him with one of the guys on the basketball team. Rick, who fell in love more times than KISS had farewell tours, was broken up about it. When Connie came in flaunting her new man in front of Rick and Ray, I couldn't stand seeing my brother hurt. I jumped up from the booth I was sitting in with my friends and grabbed the first thing in front of me, my chocolate shake, and dumped it all over her. Of course, it turned into an all-out brawl, with hair pulling and the works. Connie ran out of Johnny's Diner with tears streaming down her face, and everyone in the crowded place cheered for me. I know, not the most mature way to handle the situation but I'd do anything for my brother. You mess with him you mess with me. Wish he was here with me now, I need him more than ever. I let out an involuntary sigh. Please don't let Ray notice.

Ray always had our back too, whether he believes it or not. Screw Jared and his cronies, Ray is family. "She had it coming." I nudge Ray back. "I'll try to refrain from any milkshake dumping." Although if Jared's there I may not be able to keep that promise.

The bell rings as Ray pushes opened the door, holding it for me like the gentleman he's always been. How the hell can someone so sweet pummel his opponent to the ground like they're mortal enemies? Maybe boxing is like politics, you love 'em one day and hate 'em the next.

Of course, Jared's family is the dirtiest of politicians. Sweet to your face and would sell your firstborn behind your back. I can't believe his father was the mayor up until he passed away five years ago. Didn't know you can ride the coat tails of someone no longer with us for that long but Jared has made a career of it. A wave of nausea flows through me. I need to erase any thoughts of Jared from my mind or I'll never hold down my food.

"See that booth right over there?" Ray points to the last booth on the left. "After we won our first little league game, Coach Carter took us all out for burgers and shakes. Rick was sitting by himself and I asked if I could sit with him. The rest is history. Beginning of an era started right there."

"Hey Johnny." Jared strolls into the diner like he's walking into the Academy Awards ceremony. He looks toward Ray and snickers. "Alert the press, celebrities on site." He smirks. "Maybe we can get a few more pictures of Ray punching kids in the face."

Nausea flows through my body the second I hear that voice. God forbid he leaves me alone for the one day that's important in growing my business.

Ray swings his head around like he just ducked from jab. "I'm free for face punching photos if you need one of me and you."

An involuntary smile graces my face. There's nothing I'd like to see more than for Ray to pummel Jared, but that's not the way we solve things as adults. Right?

I turn toward Ray and nudge him closer to the booth. Jared wants a rise out of him and this time he's not getting what he wants. "Well, another new era starts right now." I clutch my papers and march toward the booth.

Ray follows, looking back at Jared as he makes his way closer. "Yeah, it's all about new beginnings." He flashes a smile, more to hide the frown that seems to appear when the reality of the situation hits him.

Rick is gone, but he lives in every part of this town. Everywhere you look is a memory you can't escape. That's pretty much why my parents moved the year after he died, right around the time I met Jared. It's near impossible to forget and move on. I'm the only idiot who thought I was in love and couldn't bear to leave Jared. Emptiness fills the pit of my stomach. How could I have been so naive?

Ray slides in the booth and runs his hand along the vinyl seat. I plop in the seat across from him, trying not to think too much or I'll burst into tears. And from the way he's acting he might too. I need to bring him back to the present.

Out of the corner of my eye, I see Jared. He shoots a death glare in our direction and leaves with a take-out order. Thank God. I drop a stack of papers on the table. The force causes a few napkins to slide around. "You should probably stretch your fingers so they don't cramp."

"My hands threw a lot of punches. Am I going to be able to do this in one sitting?" He winks. "If not, guess it'll be dinner next time."

Heat flushes across my cheeks. I'm sure they're a hundred shades of scarlet. Is he being nice or hitting on me? Dear God, what am I thinking? Like it matters. The last thing I need in my life is more complications. Even if my all-time crush is finally asking me out on a date like I dreamed of forever.

"Let's see how far we get." Okay, not the best response but it's better than jumping across the table and tackling him like every ounce of my being wants to do.

I always put the *sign here* stickers on all of my client's paperwork. It makes things easier and I don't have to hear the question "Where do I sign?" every five seconds. I turn to page three. "Sign and date here." I hold up a finger. "Did you want to read through anything first? Even though I'm sure your attorney has checked the paperwork."

"I trust you, Lys." He signs and looks up at me, his gaze burning a hole in my soul.

I turn to the next page, steading my trembling hand. If he keeps this up I'll have a thousand papercuts before we order drinks. I flip through and he signs away. The whole deal is all cash, and since Ray and Lou Johnson, the Kraken's original owner, went through the sales agreement with a fine-tooth comb, Lou signed with his witness in New York and Ray signs here with me as his witness. Since the two, along with their lawyers, agreed on these terms, after today, it's a done deal. A weird deal, but final none-the-less.

I point to the last page. He signs and clicks his pen closed. "That's it?"

"Quicker than our waitress." He nods over at Rachelle Brown, another Filmore High alumni who's juggling a mortgage, two kids, and a cheating ex-husband trying to take every penny she earns. What is it with the guys in this town? Ray must be the only half-way decent one. Dear God, please don't let the curse of Sunset Cove fall upon him.

She looks up and sees us staring at her. "Be right there." She almost drops the tray with the five glasses and two platters on it.

Dammit, I didn't mean to rush her. "Hi, Rachelle. Take your time." I wave.

Ray pulls a laminated menu from the slot attached to the wall and hands it to me. "Burgers and shakes or you want to browse?"

I take the menu and shove it back in the slot. "How can you order anything else?" Johnny's Diner is known for it's burgers and shakes. There's a whole wall of celebrities who traveled through and took their picture with Johnny, every one of them holding a shake. It's sacrilege to order anything else.

Rachelle jogs over out of breath. She grabs a pen from behind her messy brown bun and pulls out a tablet. "What'll you have?" She looks up and almost jumps back. "Ray Wilson, right?"

He nods. "In the flesh." He rubs his chin. "Rachelle, right? From Filmore High?"

She chuckles, pretty much like every girl who comes in contact with Ray seems to do, and tips her chin toward him. "Yeah, didn't think you knew who I was back then…or now."

"Of course I remember. Great to see you. We'll have two cheeseburgers and two chocolate shakes."

"It'll be right out." She jots down the order and scurries away.

"Smooth." I rest my chin on my hand and tap my fingers along my cheek. "You don't remember her at all, do you?"

He nods. "Sure I do. I just didn't remember her name until you said it." He nibbles his lip, just like Rick did every time he was lying.

"Bullshit."

He jerks his head back. "What did you say?"

"You and Rick were always the worst liars. That's why I kicked your ass in the card game, Bullshit."

"Huh, and I thought you were psychic or something." He sits back and stretches his arms.

I follow the movement of every muscle. His body flows like it's following a choreographed dance. Dear God, how can a human have that many muscles in their arms?

Rachelle steps in and breaks my trance. "Burgers will be a minute or two." She slides the shakes in front of us and takes off.

Ray sips his. His eyes light up like a kid's on Christmas morning. "Nectar of the gods."

I sip mine and get a brain freeze. I hold my hand to my forehead. "Worth the pain." I drop my hand back down to the table.

"Guess you're better at dumping them."

I roll up my straw paper and toss it at him.

He takes another sip and sits back. "So what's your story? You're Alyssa Higgins now? Like the mayor?"

Great. A trip down memory lane. It's times like this I wish I had amnesia. I take a deep breath and slowly exhale. I'll give him the short version.

I shrug. "It's not that exciting of a story. I met Jared at

Sunset Cove Community College. My parents were packing up to move and I had the choice of going with them or staying. I decided to stay to finish up my associates degree." I sip my chocolate shake, letting the icy sensation fill my mind with sweetness rather than regret.

"Can't blame them. I wouldn't have been able to stay…if I was here in the first place like I should've been." Ray looks down, his eyes empty.

I put my hand over his. "You got to let it go. Even if you were here it wouldn't change anything. Who knows, it could've been worse. You could both be gone." I look down at my hand on his and quickly take mine away. What am I thinking? Every eye in the diner has been on us since we walked in. No reason to give them dirt to gossip about. The joy of living in a small town: no one can mind their own business.

He looks up at me, his eyes locking with mine. "Doesn't matter. I should've been there."

Rachelle struts over, putting a cheeseburger platter in front of each of us. "You guys need anything else?"

Ray shakes his head.

"No thanks." I flash a smile. Got to hand it to her, she has perfect timing. Maybe she can read people from waitressing here for so long or maybe divine intervention is on my side.

Ray jerks his head as if to bring him into to reality. "So back to you. You stayed after your parents left?"

So much for changing the subject. I nod. "I finished school, got married. It didn't work out, and here we are." I smile and bite a huge chunk of my cheeseburger.

Ray grabs his and takes a mouthful. "Oh my god," he

mumbles in between chewing. "How the hell did I forget how good these taste?"

"Really? You lived in Vegas for years. Don't they have every cuisine known to man?" Five star restaurants don't exist in Sunset Cove.

"Not this." He finishes the burger in three more bites. "The Kraken had the best crab cakes that exist. I negotiated with Lou to get the recipe." He wipes the ketchup off of his lip with a napkin.

I lean back in my seat, an involuntary smile forming on my face. "The Kraken was the place to be. I literally went there after every major moment of my life. Prom, graduation, the first time I…"

He holds back a smile. "Same here. This town needs the Kraken, hell…I need the Kraken."

I scrunch my eyebrows. "Why are you back? I mean, I get it, you want to go back to your hometown but why did you retire? There're lots of boxers older."

He rubs his chin. "Don't register me for my AARP card yet."

Oh my god, what am I doing? That was beyond rude. "I'm sorry, it's really none of my business." I gather the papers into a pile and shove them back into my oversized purse.

He holds up his hand. "No worries. I'm having some health issues." He points at his right eye. "A few more hits and I'll lose my vision. Figured I'd quit while I'm ahead."

Good advice, even though an injury forcing you to quit what you love is a hard pill to swallow. Most people keep on going, thinking they're going to beat the odds. I guess Ray is a realist.

"Owning a restaurant is far from retiring." I nibble on the pen I didn't realize I was holding.

"I'm up for the challenge. I need something new. And the Kraken is legendary." He finishes his shake, slurping the last of it through his straw. "I got the cooking and management plan down, I just need to figure out how I'm going to make it the place to be again."

"I can help. I took a slew of marketing classes." I press my lips together trying to will them to stay shut. What am I thinking? I can't be working on reanimating the Kraken with Ray… or with anyone else for that matter. I need to focus on Sunset Reality, my real estate business.

"Really? I'd love some help if you've got the time. Are you free for coffee tomorrow? Maybe we can create a killer plan." His face lights up like the Rockefeller Christmas tree.

Everything about this spells trouble. I will regretfully decline but wish him the best and refer him to Beth Jones. She writes ads for the local newspaper. I'm sure she can give him some great ideas.

I lift my gaze and lock eyes with him. The blue hue instantly pierces my soul. I open my mouth to give him my speech. "Sure, sounds great."

Wait, what just came out of my mouth?

2
REVIVAL

THANK YOU GOD FOR HELPING ME REMEMBER MY sunglasses. I stare at Ray, leaning against his blue Corvette on the other side of the road. His gray shirt clings to his body, the soft ocean breeze perfectly pressing it against his chiseled muscles. My gaze shifts from his flawlessly sculpted biceps to the outline of his pecs. Didn't people once pray to statues that looked like him? I don't blame them, everything about him is divine. I take a deep breath, and slowly exhale. I wave at Ray and cross the road to meet him at the Sunset Café. Just what I need for my already jittery body: coffee.

How exactly did I get myself into this? Oh right, the whole not keeping my mouth shut issue. Well, I'll give him some pointers to help with the Kraken and then go on my merry way. He's going to do fine. The Kraken always sold itself. It was the place to be.

My mind drifts back to happier times. I had my first kiss outside the Kraken. Bobby Jenson took me there for a sundae and a walk on the beach. The second we stepped outside, he tucked a few stray hairs blowing from the ocean breeze behind my ear and grabbed both of my cheeks, kissing me like they do in romance movies. The best kiss of my life happened when I was thirteen and two months later, Bobby's dad got a job in New York City and they moved away. Who knew, the romance ends at puberty?

Ray stands up the minute I'm within a few feet of him. He slides his sunglasses from his eyes to the top of his head. Chills flow through my body the second he lets those baby blues out. He sweeps my body from my head to my toes. "Were you always this gorgeous?"

I let out a chuckle. Dammit, how can he turn me into a teenager with one glance? "Good morning to you, too."

"After you." He places his hand in the small of my back and guides me inside.

A kaleidoscope of butterflies swarms in my stomach the second he touches me. It's been forever since I reacted this way to a man. Probably because I was married to one that I grew to hate for five years. Why do I feel the same way I do when an actor jumps in front of me in a haunted house?

Ray pulls out a chair for me at a small table in the back of the restaurant. Private and cozy, exactly what we need…or maybe not. I breathe in the scent of fresh ground coffee beans. It invigorates my senses. I clear my mind and pull out my laptop.

"Wow, I was kind of thinking of a throwing a Grand Opening party or something. Nothing technical." He scoots his chair over to mine as I fire up the computer.

The scent of his musky cologne sends chills through me.

Or maybe it's the fact that there's only about three feet of space between us. Why do I remember that cologne?

My mind races backward like it stepped into a time machine to Christmas morning when I was a freshman at Filmore High. Rick ripped open his presents in warp speed just like he did since he was five years old and managed to spill the cologne Santa left in his stocking all over Mom's new rug. Woodland Creek cologne was the popular one all the guys wore back in the day. Mom wasn't thrilled her carpet smelled like it until she sold the house.

I let out a chuckle.

"What? Is it my savvy computer skills?" He slides his fingers along bottom of the laptop trying to move the cursor.

"Still wearing Woodland Creek?" I smile.

"Hell, yeah. Got to keep the ladies happy." He laughs. "Rick and I should've owned the company for how much of this stuff we bought. Guess it's sentimental, like a part of me now."

I sigh. Amazing how something you completely forgot about can flood your mind with memories. How does Ray do it? Every time he talks about Rick he's happy, almost like they're reminiscing their glory days. The second thoughts of Rick flood my mind, a brick forms in my stomach.

Doesn't matter, I'm here to get the Kraken going. I pull up the website and logo I put together last night. "Advertising is all on the web and social media. I made a quick website and Facebook page to get you started."

"Jesus, Lys. This is amazing." He runs his fingers along the orange Kraken hanging onto the words Kraken Bar and Grill.

"Thanks." So this is what it's like to be appreciated.

When I tried to revamp Jared's site for one of his many failed businesses, Higgin's Industries, he threw my laptop against the wall and told me I've ruined his reputation. Asshole.

"I was thinking we could add a picture of you standing at the bar and maybe hang a few of your boxing photos along the walls. We can add the pictures to the website along with the menu and hours. Maybe something cool like a cocktail of the week or a weekly special." I shift my gaze from the computer screen to his eyes, which look like their either dazzled or ready to shoot the fires of hell.

He raises a hand and I instantly duck. Oh God. I close my eyes, trying to fight back tears and plaster on a smile instead.

"Lys, you okay?"

I nod.

He scrunches his eyebrows and stares at my face as if he's trying to read my mind. Heat flushes across my cheeks. Please don't let him ask why I reacted in that way. I'm sure he knows.

He moves slowly, and swings an arm around my shoulder, pulling me into a side hug. "I love it, all of it. You and I make a great team, you know that?"

I flash a meek smile.

He pulls his hand away. "I'm going to reopen the back deck too. Maybe we can get a few pictures from the beach. How are your photography skills?"

I hold up my iPhone. "This is as good as it gets."

"Great, better than mine. You up for taking some photos and adding them to the site?" He runs a hand along his the back of his neck. "God, I'm sorry Lys. How much do you charge for this?"

"You're family." Did that just come out of my mouth? It is the truth though.

He shakes his head. "Nope, I'm hiring you." He taps his chin with his pointer finger. "I'll go with my manager's rate. It's pretty much the same thing."

I hold up my hands. "Ugh. It's one-hundred-percent not the same thing."

He shrugs. "Too bad. It's happening."

It's not like I can't use the money, I really need it but taking it from Ray seems so…wrong. "Let's see what you think of my work first."

He gives me a military salute. "Aye aye, captain."

The second Ray stands up, a small mob of people rush toward him like a freight train. "Ray, good to have you back. Can't wait for the Kraken to open back up," a menagerie of voices yell through the crowd of about twelve.

"Great to be back. Lys and I are going to make the Kraken better than ever. Grand Opening in a few weeks."

My heart pounds in my chest. Oh God, it's just a matter of time before Jared gets wind of me and Ray working together. Then what?

I swallow hard and push the negative thoughts to the depths of my soul. I'm done living under Jared's realm of fear. When he hears I'm working with Ray, he'll have to deal with it. We're done, and now it's legal. He can't rule me anymore, but he can make trouble, and stirring up shit is his specialty. I plaster on a smile and stand next to Ray.

Ray waves to the crowd. A few of them pat him on the back. The town reacts the same way they did to Rick back in the day when he won a big football game. The two heroes of

Sunset Cove. Ray was more behind the scenes with boxing. He had to travel a lot but the second he came back it was like a rock star graced us. Now we're down to one hero.

Ray places his arm in the small of my back and leads me out of the coffee shop the same way he led me in while the small crowd watches. Do they think I'm his groupie?

I've been called worse. I clutch the strap of my laptop case and stand up tall. Everyone can see we're working together; who knows, maybe being with Ray can open up some more business opportunities for me.

We step out of the coffee shop, leaving the crowd behind us. The sun beats down upon my face, warming my skin. I close my eyes for a minute and take in the bright rays. It's a perfect day here in Sunset Cove, calm wind, sun, and not a cloud as far as the eye can see. It's a photographer's dream.

Ray walks over toward the passenger side of his convertible Corvette and holds open the door. "Your chariot awaits."

Yeah, I don't know about this. "Shouldn't we meet at the Kraken? My car's over there." I point to my silver Toyota across the street. Since Ray's been back, I've eaten lunch with him, had coffee with him, and now I'm heading to the Kraken with him, all in less than twenty-four hours. I'm not so sure I should be jumping into a car with him too. Or spending time alone with him, for that matter.

"The car will be fine. Come on, you'll love the wind in your hair." He gestures for me to get in.

I'm sure it'll be one of the many things of I love. Great, I'm out of excuses. I shift my sunglasses from the top of my head to my eyes and walk to the car, sliding into the hot leather seat. I finagle with my dress, shoving it between the seat and the back of my thighs. If I burn myself, he'll probably talk me into letting him hold ice on it and I'd comply. God, why does my mind go blank whenever he's near me?

He closes my door and hops into the driver side. He fires up the engine and points toward the radio. "Be kind to my ears."

Ray and Rick were the biggest rock fans. They'd sing at the top of their lungs, which was painful for the rest of us in the house. Doubt he knows it, but I've seen Ray fight before. *Welcome to the Jungle* is his entrance music. I guess he doesn't remember that I'm more of a hardcore rock fan than Rick. I've got this.

I flip through the channels until I come to a classic rock station. *Paint it Black* by the Rolling Stones blasts through the speakers. It's a real oldie but a goodie, and the Stones still rock.

"Were you always this cool?" Ray turns toward me, his hand outstretched on the steering wheel.

Is he serious? He's literally the epitome of cool. "I was even more fun back in the day." Dear God, that may have been the sluttiest thing I've said in years. I adjust my sunglasses and run a hand through my hair. It'll probably look like a seagull nested in it by the time we reach the Kraken, but riding in a convertible with a hot guy was on my bucket list about fifteen years ago. Here I am, knocking it off.

Ray presses the gas and we hit the road. The salty air caresses my face, blowing strands of my hair to and fro. Music fills the air and a faint aroma of Woodland Creek cologne sweeps through. It's perfect.

The short ride to the Kraken feels like it takes a minute, rather than ten. Ray pulls into the parking lot and snags the front spot with the orange Kraken painted on the asphalt that everyone tried for back in the day. Now it's faded and parts of it are missing. Doesn't matter. It just needs a little TLC and rejuvenation to get back to its former glory. Emptiness flows through me for a second. I guess the orange Kraken and I are kindred souls.

Ray shuts down the engine and steps out of the car, coming around to my side before I can even get my hand on the handle. He opens the door for me. "Just like you remember?"

Okay, I live here so I pass by the Kraken every so often when I feel like taking a ride to the edge of town. I get it, there's nothing else around and really no reason to come here other than to run away for a bit. Nothing I'm willing to share with Ray.

"It's going to be so much better." I run my fingers through the tangled strands of my hair, trying to make it look semi-presentable and slide my sunglasses to the top of my head. I peek into the side mirror and glance at myself. Eh, not as bad as I expected and definitely worth it.

We walk up the wooden steps and Ray pulls out a menagerie of keys. I chuckle. "Are you moonlighting as a janitor?"

"I do it all, babe." He finds the key and opens up the door. "Lou must've had a different key for every door. One of the things we'll work on." He takes off his sunglasses and tucks them in the neck of his T-shirt.

I pull out a small note pad. "It's on the list."

"Add this too." Ray grabs my hand and drags me forward

like the place is on fire. "Right here is the reason I bought the place."

We head out the door in the back of the restaurant to the beach deck overlooking the ocean. I gasp and look around at the remains of the place that holds so many memories. Worn wood, chipped pain flakes, it's like I'm touring the site of ancient ruins. I stop for a minute and glance around, instantly transported back to better days. An involuntary smile graces my face.

A canopy of lights shined through the dark nights, and the sound of the waves crashing complemented the awesome bands that played on Friday and Saturday nights. Everyone was dancing around without a care in the world and singing like no one else can hear. Nothing else like it existed here or in the neighboring towns. The Kraken's deck was one of a kind. The dance floor was always filled, and a tiki bar complete with two-person swings around it made you feel like you were on a tropical island. A great escape for the night.

I never realized how much I need the Kraken until right now. We've got to bring it back to its former glory. The town needs it...I need it. Ray must feel the same way. Could this be why he moved back and bought the Kraken? I mean, he's starting over after a devastating blow, just like me.

No need for formal notes. This is a roll-up-your sleeves kind of project. I tuck my notebook into my back pocket. "We've got to bring it back, Ray." Dear God, what just came out of my mouth? I mean, this is Ray's business, not mine. I'm his hired help, not his partner. Does the Kraken have some kind of spell on me, or is it Ray? Note to self, *think before speaking*.

"Exactly." He takes a few steps toward me. Tingles sweep through me the closer he gets. He faces me and grabs both my hands.

The soft ocean breeze grazes our skin and the crashing waves provide a perfect melody. My heart pounds and a kaleidoscope of butterflies swarm in my stomach. I know I should turn away and stop whatever is about to happen but my feet are rooted to the ground. I moisten my lips with my tongue and try to keep my body from trembling. Ray moves closer and presses his forehead against mine. I close my eyes and take a deep breath. This is really happening.

"Lys?"

Acid burns through my ears, pulling me out of this perfect moment. A spine-tingling chill sweeps from my head to my feet. The sound of that voice kills any happiness that exists. My stomach drops to the floor. What the hell is he doing here?

3
FESTIVAL OF CLAMS

I JUMP BACK A MILE, CREATING AS MUCH SPACE AS I CAN between Ray and I. "Jared, I didn't know you'd be here."

He scans me from head to toe. His face looks the same way it did when we watched a scene where a zombie ripped apart someone's flesh in the *Day of the Dead*. His face is scrunched like he's about to hurl…except for his eyes. They could shoot hell-fire right through me.

"Obviously." Jared walks up to Ray holding a badge that looks like it was made by a twelve-year-old. "Jared Higgins, Zoning Inspector."

Ray holds out his hand. "Oh yeah, I remember you from Johnny's." Ray hesitates for a minute. "Nice to meet you. I'm bringing the old girl back to her former glory." Ray looks over at the Kraken and then back at Jared.

Jared turns toward me, shooting me a look of death, and then focuses back on Ray. "Yeah, I see that."

Ray jerks his head back like he can't believe someone can

be such an asshole. "What can I help you with?" Ray drops his hand to his side and stands up tall.

Dear God, is there going to be a brawl right here? Not a chance. Jared's not stupid enough to fight Ray. I mean, besides the fact Ray's a former professional boxer, Jared knows of Ray's reputation on the street. No one could take him down. After a few people who thought they were Thor fought Ray and got their ass kicked, the others stopped trying.

"Just making my rounds. Wanted to let you know any additions, fences, decks need to go through the zoning office." Jared looks around the property and then back at Ray.

"Duly noted. My building permit is in the window." Ray points to the bright orange paper that could probably be seen from space. "I'm keeping the Kraken vintage, just the way she was. No new additions, but thanks for stopping by." Ray takes a step forward.

Jared flinches. Good for the son of a bitch. It's about time someone intimidates him. He's a totally different person when his group of cronies isn't by his side. I stand tall and stare laser-beams at his body. A rush of adrenaline flows through me. So this is what's like to stand up to a bully. Why do I feel like Wonder Woman when Ray's next to me?

"Good luck," Jared mutters under his breath and high tails it out.

Carnival music floats through the air, lightening the hardest of hearts. The sun shines down, warming my skin and sending waves of energy all around. It's been years since I attended the Festival of Clams. Hiding from the town folks is sometimes easier than explaining things. Plus, Jared made up his own version of everything that went down, and for some reason he can do no wrong in this town. Doesn't matter. I'm done worrying about what people think, and missing out on things I love. This is supposed to be my fresh start. I take a deep breath and slowly exhale. Plus, I'm a hired employee of Ray, and promoting the Kraken at the biggest event of the summer is required.

I carry a big orange kraken over to Ray's booth and set it down on the counter next to the hanging nets and strategically placed starfish. "I think we're all set. How's the food coming?"

Ray cracks his knuckles. "I followed Lou's recipe exactly." He paces the length of the booth.

I squint and tip my chin. "You okay?"

He nods. "I feel the same way I do right before a big fight. Psyched up and ready to puke."

"I doubt even the best marketing expert can sell your food after you do that." Especially since every booth is required to have a clam element to their dishes. Everyone would think there's a red tide or some kind of seafood plague.

"I'll be fine. Once the festival official starts and I serve my first crab cake sandwich, I'll calm down." He nibbles his fingernails. "The booth looks great. Maybe I should hire you as my interior decorator too."

I've been dreaming of how I'd decorate a booth since I was eight years old—netting, starfish, the required clam, and a mermaid. Okay, so the mermaid was replaced with a man eating octopus, aka the kraken, but not everything always goes the way you plan.

"Thanks." I glance around at the booths lining the perimeter of the pavement which is a mammoth parking lot all the other days of the year. Mr. Jones donates it to the festival and closes up the small mall for the day. To make it worth his while, he gets to sample as much food as he'd like, free of charge.

White lights grace the trees along the sidewalk and the aroma of cotton candy fills the air. A man sets his megaphone on the stand in the middle of the festival, boasting a huge stuffed animal to anyone who can knock over all three milk bottles. Rick won me a giant unicorn every year. I take a deep breath and slowly exhale, pushing those memories to the depths of my soul.

I turn to Ray, who looks green. Dear God, he's got to pull it together. "I hop over to the other side of the booth where the customers will line up. "Okay, let's do this."

He shrugs.

"Sir, I'd like a crab cake sandwich and a dozen steamed clams please." I tap my fingers on the counter of the booth.

He stops pacing like a lion and lowers his eyebrows, staring at me. He leans his elbows on the booth. "You don't have to do this."

"I'm your first customer and I'd like to try the crab cake sandwich and a dozen clams." I pull a twenty-dollar-bill from my pocket.

He stands up tall. "Okay, you can be the official Kraken Bar and Grill taste tester…but I'm not taking your money. Let's say it's part of your job." He turns around and fills one of the plastic plates adorned with a Kraken printed on the bottom. Half-price online and perfect for this event.

The outline of the muscles in his back dance, almost bursting through the fabric of his fitted orange shirt as he prepares the food. My heart races. No matter what it tastes like, if the female public has that view he will sell out in an hour.

"Order up." He places it on the counter in front of me and folds his arms around his chest. He nibbles his thumb nail.

I grab the crab cake sandwich and take a huge bite, setting the rest back down on the plate. Dear God, it's like going back in time. A perfect clone of what once existed.

I take in the savory flavors and I'm transported back to the eighth grade. Mom and Dad took Rick and I to the Kraken almost every Friday night for dinner. It was our family night out. Well, right after school was out and I was about to become a freshman at Fillmore High, I decided to try something other than chicken fingers and fries. Alas, my first taste of the Kraken's crab cake. This is a dead ringer for the original.

"Better than sex." Oh my God, did I just say that out loud? I quickly swallow the remaining food in my mouth, although I should probably keep it full for fear of saying something else equally inappropriate.

He snickers. "I was going for edible but I like the way you think." He drops his arms to his sides and grabs the rest of the sandwich from my plate. He takes one bite, devouring almost half of it. His tense muscles relax the moment he starts chewing. "Pretty close to what you said." He finishes the rest of the sandwich.

"You've got this, Ray." I duck underneath the booth to the service side and grab a bottle of water from my bag. A stack of papers glide up on my knuckles. Right, I didn't even get a chance to talk to Ray about my out-of-the-box marketing idea. I swig my water and set it on the counter. Well, he's in a pretty good mood at the moment, let's see what he thinks.

I take the papers from my bag and hold them to my chest. "I've got a marketing idea I want to run by you. It's exciting, will gather a crowd, and personalized to you."

He throws away the dirty plate and faces me, giving me his full attention. "Let's hear it."

"Keep an opened mind." Why am I making this seem like I'm trying to sell him the worst idea in the world? He's not anti-boxing. I mean, he only retired because he had to, not because he hates the sport all of a sudden. "When Ray the Wrecker comes back to town, what do people want?"

He shrugs.

"A hero…and that's how the town feels about you."

He scrunches his eyebrows, causing a dimple to appear in his cheek when he tries to hold back a smile. "Lys, you're crazy. Everyone knows I'm no Superman. Just a guy who got lucky, that's all."

"I think there was a lot more skill involved. Rick always said, you move like a cheetah and strike like a cobra." I set one of the flyers I made on the counter. "How do you feel about hosting an amateur event?"

He walks to the counter and leans over, reading the flyer like a lawyer going through a document with a fine-tooth comb.

I search his face, but his chiseled jaw line and to-die-for blue eyes suck me in so deep I can't read his expression. I blink repeatedly, trying to pull myself out of the whirlpool of Ray's charm.

"I already got all the permits required for an outdoor sports event. Sunset Reality sponsored a volleyball tournament two years ago, so I'm versed in this type of event. I think it will bring a huge crowd to the Kraken and it's better than any grand opening I've ever attended. Plus, this is what the town wants, to bring a little Las Vegas to Sunset Cove." Okay Lys, shut up and stop babbling. You sound like a used car salesman.

He grabs the flyer and faces me. "This…" he holds it out to me, "is amazing. Fight Night at the Kraken."

An ear-to-ear smile spreads across my face. I exhale the breath I didn't realize I'd been holding. "Nothing like this has been done in Sunset Cove before. I think it's going to be huge."

Ray runs a hand through his hair, slicking back the brown locks. "I can hang up my belt and a few boxing photos from my glory days. We can set up the ring right on the beach past the deck. That way people can sit on the deck, have their drinks, and watch." He pulls me into a hug, pressing his impressive body against mine.

I'm breathless. Not sure if it's from his hold on my body or the fact he's so close to me not even air can get in between us. "I'm so happy you're onboard."

"Are you kidding? Everything about this is perfect." He relaxes his hold and takes a step back. "I'll have one of my friends ref the fight and I'll be the ring announcer. I can even have a few of my boxing buddies be judges." He almost floats around the booth, like a weight has been lifted from his body.

I guess the nervous energy disappeared. Amazing how

stress vanishes when you're back to doing something you love. I set up a picture frame with a promo poster for Fight Night, some flyers, and a sign-up sheet for anyone who wants to jump in the ring next to the Kraken on the counter.

Marketing the Kraken's reopening, the resurrection of the unforgettable food, and an amateur boxing event all at the Festival of Clam's booth. What the hell am I thinking?

A mob of people storm through like a tidal wave. It's go-time; the festival has begun. Oh my god, I almost forgot. I toss an orange T-shirt to Ray. "More marketing." How could I overlook the shirts I had made for the festival? Everyone knows a T-shirt is a walking billboard and when a huge kraken graces the back, you remember it.

Ray holds up the shirt. "Lys, you're unbelievable. I mean, if you managed a rock band you'd sell out stadiums." He pulls up the hem of his shirt and slides it over his head.

My heart just about beats out of my chest and flies around through the air. I follow the path of the fabric, gliding over the peaks and valleys of his perfectly chiseled body. My mouth falls opened. Dear God, if Helen of Troy's face launched a thousand ships Ray's body could summon a million.

He puts on the Kraken shirt, which fits his body like a glove. He runs a hand through his hair and looks down and his shirt before gazing up at me. "What do you think?"

If this is remotely what heaven is like I'll read the bible every day to make sure I'm in. "Best view in the whole festival." I gasp. Oh god, I said that out loud. I put my hand over my mouth, trying to hold in any other inappropriate comments. Heat spreads across my cheeks like wildfire. I take a breath and drop my hand to my side. "I mean…I think these shirts are great advertising for the Kraken. I had one hundred made; maybe we can give some out tonight. Good, I'll bring this conversation back to marketing the Kraken.

"Thanks." He flashes a half-smile and winks.

Dammit, caught red-handed.

"What's this about?" Jared's voice drips with sarcastic laughter. "Seriously, no one even follows boxing anymore."

"Sheet's right here if you want to sign up. I'd love to teach you a few things." Ray's chiseled jaw bulges as he grinds his teeth.

"No lessons needed, thanks." He slides the flyer across the counter.

"Wasn't offering them." Ray folds his arms across his chest. His biceps flex so hard I can see his veins popping.

As much as I'd love to see Ray pummel Jared to oblivion, I've got to stop this before it gets out of hand. We're here to get the Kraken off its feet, not to end Jared's reign of terror.

"What do you need, Jared?" I wedge myself between Ray and the counter, staring the fires of hell into Jared's eyes. If I only had the courage to do it two years ago, my life would be a hell of a lot different, but then again courage comes easy when there's a boxing champion backing you up.

"Checking on all the local businesses. Part of my job." Jared flashes his ridiculous zoning officer badge. Seriously, it's not an FBI identification, even though he thinks he's part of the damn secret service. "I take it you have all the necessary permits for this…event."

"You've got a lot of…" Ray stops the second I look into his eyes and shake my head.

"Yes. Sunset Reality is sponsoring the event and has all the permits." I bend down and grab my folder from the box near the back of the booth. I made all the copies in the event Jared tried to push around his authority. I've got his number down.

Jared eyes travel from my head to my feet, his lips curl downward. "I'm sure Sunset Reality is doing a hell of a lot more than that."

Ray takes two steps forward, only the thin countertop separating him from Jared. He points his finger in Jared's face. "What did you say to her?"

Jared shrugs. "She's expanding her business."

"We both know that's not what you meant." Ray presses his lips together in a tight line.

Jared holds up his hands. "Whatever. Take it how you want." He doesn't come any closer but glances at the promo poster. "Hope you don't plan on bringing any more hot-headed boxers to Sunset Cove. We wouldn't want any problems in our perfect town." He flashes a cocky smile.

"Everything we're doing is to better the town, Jared. Maybe you should help with that by leaving. Then Sunset Cove would be the best place in the world." I fold my arms across my chest and glare at him.

He rolls his eyes. "Maybe if you could keep your legs closed for five minutes we'd have a better class of ladies here."

Ray jumps over the counter in one swoop and charges toward Jared. Oh God, he's egging him on to ruin him. I sprint between the two and wrap my arms around Ray's neck. It's the only way to prevent this from turning into a shit-show. Okay, so maybe getting in the middle of a guy fight with a professional boxer and the biggest asshole in the world is about as smart as getting in the middle of a dog fight. Doesn't matter,

I can't let Jared bring Ray down like he did to me and half of the town. He's not going to win this time.

Jared lunges backward the second Ray comes at him and falls on his ass. A few people walking by chuckle, and a split second later his cronies show up. Jared gets up once his posse is next to him and pats the dirt off his jeans. "You better watch yourself."

"Ditto," Ray yells.

I slowly slide my hands down Ray's neck, taking in the woodsy aroma of his cologne. Tingles sweep through me. It's like the world stands still and only the two of us exist. The pop of a balloon brings me back to reality. I jump, creating distance between me and Ray. I point at the line forming at the Kraken booth. We walk toward the line of people, Ray turning back to stare down Jared on more time before returning to the booth.

I plaster on my million-dollar smile and duck underneath the counter to man the booth. Ray follows suit. We need to blow off the confrontation with Jared and focus on the task at hand: marketing the Kraken.

"He's just trying to get under your skin. Ignore him, he gets off on taking people down." I grab a paper menu and place it on the counter.

"If he wants me, he can have me…in the ring."

4

RED TAPE

I nibble my lip as I pull my car over in front of a charming Cape Cod house. The yellow siding and light blue shutters scream *beach home* and the wraparound porch makes you feel like you're in the country. It's the perfect combination of all the things I love, pretty much my dream house.

I've only been here once before. It was Ray's graduation party. His parents hosted a backyard barbeque, and Rick insisted I come and see how the cool kids party. He delivered; it was one of the best nights of my life. Dancing, a band that could have rivaled Guns N' Roses, a bonfire, and great company. Days like that are extinct. Amazing how Ray seems to be in all my best memories. Weird coincidence?

I scan red and yellow tulips lining the perimeter of the sidewalk and follow the cobblestone path to the wraparound porch that would make Norman Rockwell jealous. Hanging flower baskets with red petunias add to the charm. It's the epitome of a postcard photo. I glance at the gingerbread woodwork. A lost art, no one wants to put in the time needed to create something amazing. Except Ray, he's pouring his heart and soul into fixing up the Kraken. He's like a renaissance era sculptor, except he could be the subject of the chiseled statue.

My heart beats faster. I take a deep breath and slowly exhale. Come on Lys, get it together. Why the hell do I act like I've never been in a room with a man before whenever I'm within three feet of Ray? I mean, I've been around him my whole life, and now I decide he's irresistible? Or maybe I always knew it.

I shake off my thoughts and try to clear my mind, focusing back on the house. I had my first beer while sitting in that white rocking chair. Of course, I downed some spiked punch afterward and ended up puking in the bushes. If I can refrain from doing that today, we'll call it a win. Well, it's now or never.

I swing open the car door, grabbing my briefcase on the way, and hop out of the car. I close the door quietly, mustering up the professional Alyssa before Ray realizes I'm here. The mountain of paperwork involved in setting up Fight Night may scare him out of town. My stomach drops to the floor. God, I hope that's not true. For the first time since Rick died, I feel alive. It's like Ray reviving the Kraken reanimated me too. It's like I'm part of something that could be great.

A sour tang invades my mouth. Jared can't stand when anyone succeeds without his involvement. He pretty much takes credit for anything good that happens in this town, and he's the first to point fingers when things go wrong. For some God knows why reason, people in this town actually believe him. Ugh, he's like Hitler.

I clench my briefcase close to me and push the vile thoughts to the depths of my stomach. Okay, time to get this show on the road. I march up the cobblestone walkway, trying to avoid falling on my face. It's been at least a year since I wore heels. These black ones with the rhinestone on the top always make me feel like I belong in New York City. A stylish, confident woman ready to take on the world.

I lift my hand to knock on the door the second Ray swings it open.

"Welcome to Casa de Wilson." He gestures for me to come inside.

I walk slowly, trying not to take a spill on the hardwood floors. He places his hand in the small of my back and guides me through the foyer to the kitchen. Tingles sweep through my body the second he touches me. I try and steady my wobbly legs. Dear God, am I going to make it through this day without bursting into flames?

The aroma of coffee fills the air. I follow the scent to a kitchen that looks so much like the one in my mom's house where I grew up. A bay window above the sink, complete with herbs in pots, French doors which lead out to the back porch, and a cute nook with a small table and four chairs. I head over to the table and rummage through my briefcase, setting the papers on the shiny surface.

Ray comes over with two cups of coffee. "Hope you like cream and sugar."

"Who doesn't?" Coffee is probably the last thing I need

and I'm more of a Splenda and skim milk kind of girl but it's nice to have someone bring you coffee. Jared expected me to wait on him like I was hired help. Of course, I tried to be the good wife and comply, but it's just another thing that made me resent him. One of about a million. I sip the coffee, and glance over at the newspaper draped almost in half at the far end of the table.

I focus on the picture on the front page. Dear God, it's me and Ray working in the Kraken stand at the Festival of Clams. My heart rate triples.

Ray slides over the paper. "Looks like we made the front the page."

All I can do is nod. Something like this will send Jared off the deep end. God, what the hell is going to pull now?

"Isn't it great, Lys. Free publicity for the Kraken. And it advertises Fight Night. Looks like we got lucky." Ray slides into the chair next to mine and sips his coffee.

I gaze at his chiseled jawline and sweet smile plastered on his face. God, he wants this so bad and doesn't realize Satan himself is trying to take him down. Who the hell am I to piss in his Cheerios? No need to tell him Jared is probably plotting to destroy Fight Night as we speak.

Time to get down to business and then I'll head to the municipal building to try and get everything passed before Jared has a chance to dig his claws in. "First, I copied all the insurance papers from the Kraken to prove we are an insured establishment…I mean you…I mean the Kraken." Dear God since when is there a "we"? I slide a lock of hair behind my ear and do my best to shake off the Freudian slip.

Ray holds back a smile.

I swallow hard, trying to push the embarrassment to the depths of my soul. "Here's a few papers to sign. Since you have a liquor license, it makes things much easier. We will need a Section 30 application for temporary structure, which will be the ring. And also a temporary event notice."

He runs a hand through his hair. "So everyone can't just show up and watch a fight?" He covers his face with his hands and runs them down his chin. "When did everything get so complicated?"

That's the million dollar question. "The second we walked off that stage holding our diplomas." Although my complications started when I married Satan.

"Lys, are we gonna be able to pull this off?"

Which part? "Yeah, it sounds worse than it is. A normal event in town attracts around five hundred people; we need to cap it at 499. I've got all the paperwork taken care of. I really just need a few signatures from you."

Ray signs in all the spots with a "sign here" sticker. He shakes his head and stands up. "How did I get so lucky to find you…I mean, if I knew back in the day what I know now, things would be different."

Chills sweep through my body, erecting every hair on my skin. I gather the paperwork into my briefcase and stand up, tightening my muscles to control my wobbly legs. "Same here." Not that I'd ever have the guts to ask Ray out and there's no way Rick would let it happen back then either.

"Rick always said his little sister is the best person alive. Guess I should've paid more attention." He turns toward me and pulls me into a hug.

My heart pounds in my chest. I wrap my arms around him and hold him close, taking in the scent of Woodland Creek and Ray. A combination that could melt the coldest heart.

He loosens his muscles and takes a step back, pressing his forehead to mine. I close my eyes, losing myself in this perfect moment. He grabs my cheeks with both hands and touches his lips to mine. My heart beats in overdrive. I weave my fingers in the strands of hair along his neck. Shockwaves flow through every ounce of my being. He slides his hands down to my waist and presses his body against mine.

The theme from Rocky blasts through the air, pulling me back to reality. I jump, breaking my lip-lock. Ray grabs his phone from the table, gives it a glance, and sets it back down.

"Not important." He tucks a stray strand of hair behind my ear.

Dear God, what am I doing? I need to get out of here and away from Ray right now, or I'll never leave. "It's okay, I have an appointment in a half-hour. I'll get this paperwork started…I mean finished. Talk to you soon." I grab my briefcase and wave while almost running to my car.

"Lys…wait."

I keep my fast pace and slide into the car, starting it up and taking off like I'm in the middle of a drag race. Once I turn the corner, I let out the breath I didn't know I was holding and slow the car to the speed limit.

What the hell happened in there? I know better than to date my employer, plus the last thing I need is to get involved with anyone right now. For God's sake, my divorce just became final. Jared, a.k.a. Satan, and would do anything to ruin any shred of happiness that might exist for me. And the thing about Jared, he'll take down anyone associated with me, too. Ray deserves better than to get caught up in Jared's revenge scheme.

But that kiss…even my toes curled. I mean, sure I've imagined kissing Ray since I was fourteen but reality was so much better than anything I could've concocted in my mind. It's like we have this bond that can't be broken by space or time.

I roll my eyes at myself. Come on, Lys. Hero's don't exist and neither does the romance you find in movies or books. It's not like Ray is the white knight and you're the girl who got away. Life doesn't work that way. Besides, maybe I make him feel like he did years ago. I'm the only bond left between him and his best friend. Could saving me resolve his issues for not being able to save Rick?

I take a few deep breaths. Okay, I'm no psychiatrist and I'm probably thinking way too much into everything. I'm the only girl he's around in town so far and he wants to have some fun. Yep, that's exactly what all of this is about. If that's true why do I want to turn the car around and speed back to him?

I pull into my driveway and turn off the engine. Ugh, how am I going to explain the way I just acted? I lean back into the headrest and rub my forehead. I'll just blow it off like it never happened. It's not like guys like to over-analyze everything. I'm sure he'll let it go. But will I be able to forget?

I pat the passenger seat for my purse. Huh, could've sworn I left it there. I lean over and toss my briefcase to the side, looking for my black leather shoulder bag. Must've fallen behind the seat. I dig my hands around the gray carpet, still nothing. I sit up and check the backseat. A blue glimpse flashes through my rear view mirror followed by the roar of an engine. The blood drains from my face. I'd know that sound anywhere.

I sigh, replaying the day's events in my mind like a broken record. How could I be so stupid? A chill sweeps through my body from my head to my toes. The blue Corvette parks on the road, blocking my driveway. Great, no escape this time.

I stare at the rearview mirror, watching Ray hop out of the car and walk up to mine. Okay, so I forgot my purse when I ran out of his house like a demon was chasing me. On some level, that couldn't be more true.

I take a deep breath and step out of the car, leaning against it to keep my balance. I wave.

"I think you forgot something." Ray slings my purse around a shoulder and stops a foot away from me.

"See, I knew it was your color and style." I flash a fake smile.

"Nah, I think brown looks better with my sneakers." He takes the purse off his shoulder and hands it to me. "House looks great."

I nod. "I've been trying to keep up on it." I dig for my keys and sling the purse around my shoulder.

"Glad I caught you before your appointment."

I nibble my lip. "Funniest thing, they cancelled the minute I got in the car."

He lowers his eyebrows. "That is weird. Especially since your phone is in your purse. I tried to call and when my table started ringing, I saw you left it."

Dammit, caught red handed. I close my eyes and hang my head down in defeat. I take a breath and raise my eyes to meet his gaze. "I had to go." The keys fall out of my trembling hand.

Ray bends down and picks them up. "What did he do to you?"

Pretty much took everything, my self-esteem, my friends, my spirit. I suck in a breath. My eyes well with tears. I blink repeatedly, stopping them from falling down my face. I will never waste another tear on Jared or anything that has to do with him. "It doesn't matter…not anymore."

Ray balls his hands into fists and slowly releases them. "Exactly. Fresh start…right?" He flashes a smile that could melt a glacier.

I nod. It's all I can do. If I open my mouth I'll probably burst into tears. Why can't I erase the Jared years from my life? He ruined me. It'll be a miracle if I ever trust another man again, even one I've known forever.

"Want a ride to the municipal building to get that paperwork going? We can be like Bonnie and Clyde." He nudges my shoulder. "Shotgun picks the music."

I let out a chuckle. Rick's favorite saying. Probably because he always rode shotgun in Ray's fancy muscle cars. Ray's dad owned the only car lot in town so Ray had his choice of vehicles. My parents were more of a station wagon family. Not the coolest wheels to be cruising around the town.

"Are we robbing banks?" I lower my eyebrows.

"We'll see where the day takes us." He puts his hand in the small of my back and guides me to the Corvette.

Tingles sweep through me from his touch. Even though

my brain wants me to steer clear of Ray, or any guy for that matter, it can't stop my body from reacting. Maybe that's what I need, my brain to shut off for a few days. God, what am I thinking?

Ray opens the passenger door and I slide into the warm leather, tucking my purse and briefcase onto the floor. He hops into the driver seat and fires up the engine. The second it turns on, I hit the buttons on the radio.

"You're quick." He shifts into drive. "Be gentle on my ears."

I flash him a smirk. Like I'd choose anything but awesome music. I head to the classic rock channel and turn up the volume the second I hear *Here I go Again* by Whitesnake.

"Nice. Are you going to slide across the hood of the car?" He winks.

I shrug. "We'll see where the day takes us." Did I just say that out loud? What am I doing? One second I'm running for the hills and the next I'm talking like some groupie at a rock concert. Nothing like giving Ray mixed signals. But that's the thing about being with Ray; we can go back to normal in two seconds flat.

He finishes the three mile drive to the municipal building a few seconds after the song ends and pulls into an empty spot. I scan the lot. Thank God, Jared's car isn't here. For once, something is working out. I grab the door handle, but Ray stops me. He gets out and comes around to the other side and opens it for me.

Sure he's a gentleman, but this seems like something more. "Are you my bodyguard?"

He holds out his hand to help me out of the car and closes the door behind me. "I'll be whatever you need me to."

My heart melts into a puddle. "I need Ray Wilson, nothing more." I slide my hand into his and we walk together.

5

FIGHT NIGHT

Whoever said a finely tailored suit on a man is the equivalent of lingerie on a woman got it right on the money. Perfectly fitted black jacket with darker lapels clinging to a mound of muscle you only see on statues of Greek Gods. Black pants that accentuate every curve just the right way, and a bow tie, with a splash of orange to represent the Kraken. I stare at Ray in awe. His slicked back hair showcases those piercing blue eyes that set my soul on fire and accentuates his strong jaw line. He's the perfect mix of bad-ass and elegant wrapped into one.

"Who's ready to rumble?" Ray walks to the middle of the boxing ring set up a few feet away from the deck of the Kraken Bar and Grill.

A massive roar of cheers fill the air. There's got to be at least five hundred people here, probably more since it's spilling out onto the beach. Most of the town's officials are here and I doubt any would have a problem with it...well, maybe one. I'm saying my Novena that Jared doesn't show up tonight.

Thunderstruck by ACDC blasts though the warm summer night. Half the crowd hums to the tune. Two guys, one in black shorts and one in red make their way to the ring with their entourage.

"Welcome everyone. The Kraken Bar and Grill presents Fight Night." Ray throws his hands in the air and the crowd cheers. "Rules are simple. Have fun, lots of food, and come back to see us again." He walks over to toward the guy in the black shorts who could be Mike Tyson's twin. "In the black corner we have Mickey 'The Mangler' Montosoro. Ten wins, two losses, three knockouts."

Ray shifts to the other fighter, a pretty boy who could pose for an Abercrombie and Fitch ad. I follow the moves of his muscles dancing under the premium fabric. "And in the red corner, Steel Sid Phillips, twelve wins, one loss, six knockouts."

"Our referee for tonight, and former middleweight champion of the wooorld...Logan Fetterman." The crowd screams like *Led Zeppelin* just jumped on the stage and is about to play a makeshift concert.

Okay, so I don't follow boxing but I guess this guy is a big deal. Doesn't matter. I can't peel my eyes from Ray. If I could create a cardboard cutout of the perfect looking man, he's standing right in front of me. Everything about him shines tonight. He's in his element. The way he works the crowd, his face glowing like a Christmas tree, the way the fighters look at him. He's meant to be in the ring, even if he's not the main event.

Ray slides under the ropes and out of the ring. He scans

the crowd and stops the second he sees me, like the Terminator when he finds his target. My heart pounds when his eyes meet mine. Dear God, how am I going to make it through this night without bursting into flames?

Ray steps his pace up to a slow jog and heads over to me. I lift my trembling hand and wave. My body temperature rises, higher with every step he takes closer to me.

"You're a genius, Lys. Look at this turnout." Ray gestures toward the ring.

Is he seriously giving me credit for this? He's got to be the most humble person I've ever met in my life. "This is all you, babe." Oh my god, did I just call him babe? My brain must be melting. "I mean…"

"Thanks." He slings an arm around me. "Babe." He lets out a chuckle.

I nuzzle my face into his chest. Didn't think he'd let that one slide. Once, Rick overheard me telling my best friend at the time, Shelley Daniels, that I thought Ray was hot and he teased me for a week. Letting slips go is not one of Rick and Ray's strong points.

Wait, what am I doing? Pretty much the whole town is here watching me flirt with Ray. I lift my head and take a step back. He lowers his eyebrows. Screw it. I move closer and rest my head on Ray's shoulder. Right now, every woman in the crowd is probably giving me death stares. Jared will have to wait in line to destroy me tonight.

"Watch this. Sid keeps dropping his hand when he jabs. Mickey's going to clock him." Ray points toward the ring.

I lift my head and focus on the fight. One of the hardest struggles in my life thus far is happening right now, taking my attention off of Ray and putting it toward the fight. I watch the two brutes battle it out and *bam,* Mikey nails Sid in the face, just like Ray predicted. A loud thump resonates through the crowd as Sid falls. Logan counts to eight and waves his hands in an X.

"Gotta go." Ray kisses my cheek and jumps back into the ring.

A million butterflies take flight in my stomach and a smile spreads across my face like wildfire. I feel like I was just crowned prom queen in front of the whole world. I press my lips together trying to contain the ear to ear smile about to burst from my face.

I watch Ray, the star of the show in my eyes. He takes the microphone and heads to his happy place, the middle of the ring.

"Winner by knockout. Mickey 'The Mangler' Montosoro." He holds up Mickey's boxing glove and the crowd goes into an all-out roar of clapping and cheers.

"Please…it was fixed." A person screams through the crowd the second the volume lulls to a quite rumble. The slurred speech doesn't cover up the worst sound I could possibly hear right now. Jared's voice.

Ray scrunches his eyebrows and shakes off the ignorant comment. He hands Mickey one of the plastic trophies we had made with a Kraken on the top holding boxing gloves, and a fifty-dollar gift card to the Kraken Bar and Grill.

I scan the crowd, looking for the vile face attached to the drunken voice but come up short. Maybe I got lucky and he passed out somewhere. I wouldn't be heartbroken if the crowd trampled him. Okay, wishing death on Jared isn't the most mature thing to be thinking about but it would make quite a few lives better, especially mine.

I stand ringside in Ray's field of vision. If anyone knows how Jared gets when he's drunk, it's me. How could I have been so stupid to stay with him for so long? I used to binge-watch Lifetime movies and criticize the women who stayed in abusive relationships until I became one of them. Now I can't even turn on the channel. Sure, there were good times but the bad ones erased them. The worse part of it all is that he made me believe I was nothing.

I look at Ray. He flashes that sexy smile the second I'm in his field of vision. Ray must tell me I'm amazing a hundred times a day; he almost has me believing it. Everything about him excites me. It's like the world is our oyster when we're together. That positive energy makes me believe anything is possible. Am I crazy, or just caught up in his spell?

"Is everyone having a good time?" Ray yells into the microphone.

Cheers erupt and I'm probably the loudest one. What am I doing? It's like I'm at a rock concert. My mind travels back to the first time I saw a band live. God, I haven't thought about it in years. Of course, Ray was there. He and Rick scored KISS tickets on one of their many farewell tours. We had third row seats. Ray got them from one of his boxing promoters back before he went pro. Three tickets and instead of inviting one of the popular girls from school who pretty much worshipped both of them, they took me. Of course, I was stoked. I painted each of our faces like the guys from the band. Rick was "the Demon", Gene Simmons' persona. Ray was "Star Man" like Paul Stanley, and I went for the Peter Kris's "Cat". One of the most amazing nights of my life, from the flawless show, and the astonishing pyrotechnics, to the best company. Tonight is a pretty close flashback, except one key ingredient is missing. Memories of Rick flooding my mind are all happy ones until the day he was gone. Why does the pain overtake it all? I breathe deep and shake off negative thoughts.

I thought the best times were behind me. Maybe I'm just getting started on a reboot. I watch Ray announce the next two fighters.

"Ready for some more rumbling?" Ray throws his hands in the air, hyping up the crowd.

I almost have to cover my ears to mute the thunderous cheers. He belongs in the ring, even if he's not the one fighting. Hasn't he ever thought about announcing or giving commentary like some of the other retired boxers? Strange, he completely left that world and went back to one from his past.

Ray interrupts my train of thought. "In the blue trunks with a record of 20 wins, 2 draws, and 16 knockouts, Juan "the Razor" Ramierez. And in the gold trunks with a record of 18 wins, 1 draw, and 17 knockouts, Ferocious Phil Fisher."

The crowd erupts like a volcano. Ray's ear-to-ear smile spreads through the crowd like a pandemic. The bell tolls. He slides out of the ring and stands next to me.

"Look at this place." I gesture to the mass of people. "Do we have enough food and alcohol to serve everyone?" Dammit, I did it again. "I mean do you?"

He slings an arm around me. "You got it right the first time."

Heat flushes through my body like a firestorm. "We" means so much more than those two letters. Ray and I together is so new, but decades old. Exciting and familiar. I pinch my arm just to make sure I'm not in the middle of an awesome dream. Ouch. Nope. All of it is real.

Ray gives a "good job" nod to one of the waitresses. A whole staff hired and trained within a week and a half and killing it on what will probably be the busiest night in the history of the Kraken. "We're all good here." He winks.

Believe me, we're more than good. Butterflies form in my stomach. Dear God, to think I almost screwed this up a few weeks ago. Eh, it's all in the past. I'm ready to take a chance on this "we" and for once, I'm not going to talk myself out of it.

A minute later, Phil knocks out Juan. Screams ring through my ears, blocking everything else. Ray jumps through the ropes the second Logan calls the fight. Blood splatters fill the floor of the ring.

My heart pounds. I close my eyes to suppress the memory that's trying to surface. The night Jared came home from his brother's bachelor party at 4 a.m. The smell of whiskey and stale cigarettes float through the air. I made the mistake of waiting up for him. He stumbled into the table and knocked over a lamp, sending shards of glass all over the hardwood floor. I should've let it go and yelled at him the next morning but I was pissed. The fact that he smelled like cheap perfume set me off like a rocket. I don't even remember what I yelled but I can't erase the rest of it from my mind. I run my finger along the scar on my bottom lip. Three stitches and blood splattered all over the tan couch.

"You still with me?" Ray stands behind me, wrapping his arms around me.

I plaster on a smile. "Yeah, just a little squeamish from the blood." It's not the time or place to tell him the truth, and I probably wouldn't anyway. I look just as bad as Jared for putting up with his bullshit. Rick's sister, nothing but a coward.

"The main event is coming up soon. Let's grab a drink. We deserve a little celebrating." He kisses my cheek and guides me toward the beach bar.

I slither through the crowd of people, tipping their plastic cups to Ray as he walks by them. The artificial palm trees on each corner of the bar almost make you feel like you're in a tropical paradise. The coconuts and tiki statues in between the bottles of alcohol boast a Hawaiian getaway. Note to self, *next event needs to be Hawaii themed*. I make my way through the three-deep crowd to the front of the bar.

I turn toward Ray. "Drinks on me." And then face the bar, pulling a twenty-dollar bill out of my pocket and waving it at the bartender.

"I don't think so." He gestures toward the bartender and she comes right over as if he cast a magical spell. "Jack and Coke for me and whatever my girlfriend wants."

I freeze, paralyzed. Wait, what did he just say? The bartender stares at me as if I have three heads. I open my mouth and blurt out the first thought in my head. "Malibu Bay Breeze, please." Okay, so my brain is still functioning. Do I pretend I didn't hear it or say something? Come on Alyssa, what are you going to say "Gee, did you just call me your girlfriend?" I'll just play it cool.

The waitress sets our drinks in front of us. I push the money toward her. She winks and nods at Ray. I sip the sweet concoction. Okay, so I guess my money is no good here. Ray's too much of a gentleman to let me pay anyway. It's a perk of being the owner's girlfriend. Heat flashes through me. Is it from the alcohol or my newfound title?

"Look at this, Lys." Ray does a 360, glancing at the crowd. "The Kraken is back."

I nod. "You did it. I never had a doubt."

"We did it." He sets down his drink and faces me.

My heart pounds in my chest the second his eyes lock with mine. He takes a step forward and lifts my chin with his index finger. Wildfire surges through me. He presses his lips to mine. The strong taste of Jack Daniels mixes with the sweet coconut bay breeze. I release my grip of the cool drink and set it on the bar. I wrap my arms around Ray's neck, weaving my fingers in the hair along his neckline. Ray presses his body against me, pinning me between him and the bar. The world around us stops for a moment.

"Ray, they're ready for you," the waitress yells.

He pulls away, catching his breath. "Duty calls."

I stand, breathless. A menagerie of eyes fill my field of vision. Really…making out in a bar at one of the biggest events in town. Way to keep everything under the radar, Lys.

Ray slams his Jack and Coke and grabs my hand, pulling me back toward the ring. I lift my cup and gulp the rest of my drink. The sweet alcohol burns my throat as it slides down. She made me a strong one. Perfect, it's exactly what I need.

Ray lets go of my hand once we're ringside and jumps under the ropes. He grabs a microphone and gets back to business like he didn't miss a beat. I stare at him as if I'm watching a rock star. He works the crowd, hyping everyone up for the main event.

"And now, the moment you've been waiting for, our main event of the evening. In the green shorts out of Boston Massachusetts, with a record of 25 wins no losses and 25 knockouts, Colin "The Crusher" Murphy."

I nibble my fingernails, looking back and forth through the crowd. What the hell is wrong with me? Why do I care who saw me and Ray making out like drunken college kids at a fraternity party? Even if Jared spotted us, he can't do a damn thing about it. For once, I'm safe. Now, if I could only get my mind to believe it.

"In the silver shorts out of Bronx, New York, with a record of 22 wins, no losses, 21 knockouts, Bruce "The Brawler" Jacobs." Ray winks at me as he passes by.

My heart flutters. I flash a smile. Anytime I'm the least bit anxious, one look from Ray and it all goes away, turning me into mush. Dammit, how can I love that then hate it all at the same time?

Ray meets both guys in the middle of the ring and they touch gloves. He steps out of the ring then comes over next to me. "Watch close, it's going to be a quick one. Colin's about to go pro."

The bell rings. The two men start to battle. Three punches in, Colin connects with an uppercut. Bruce falls to the ground. Logan does an eight count and stops the fight. Knockout.

Ray kisses my cheek. "Gotta go." He jumps back into the ring grabbing the microphone.

"Bullshit. It's fixed," a voice screams through the crowd.

Half the patrons look around to look for the one who keeps running his mouth.

"Come up here, you'll be next," Colin screams.

Jared just can't keep his mouth shut. I hope he keeps it up. There's nothing I want to see more than Colin pummeling him.

I scan the crowd but no sign of him. Maybe someone finally escorted him out. Thank God. He has no business being here. I don't even finish the thought when I see Jared emerge from the crowd.

My heart races and my mind regresses back to when we were together. I turn to run but the sea of people prevent me from getting very far. Jared comes at me like a freight train. Ray spots him and jumps out of the ring as if he's a professional wrestler rather than a boxer. Jared pushes me, knocking me to the ground. I roll in my protective ball, to prevent my face and organs from being attacked.

Ray rips Jared off of me and flings him. I peek over a shoulder and see Jared's body knocked against the ring like a ragdoll. Jared stays down for a few seconds and then jumps back up.

"Go ahead, I'll sue you for everything you've got," Jared slurs.

Ray's relaxes his hands, now balled into fists. Thank God, he stopped. He gets it; Jared would take everything if Ray beats him to oblivion.

"You're not worth it," Ray screams to Jared.

"She's not worth it," Jared says.

He moves forward and takes a swing at Ray. Ray ducks. Jared tries again, and Ray moves like he's in The Matrix. The crowd laughs. Ray does his boxer dance, swaying back and forth every time Jared tries to connect a shot. Ray hypes up the crowd, pointing to his chin. Jared swings so hard he misses and falls over. The crowd claps and laughs.

Not that Ray needs it, but one of the bouncers he hired to control the crowd makes his way to us and escorts Jared out.

"This isn't over," Jared yells.

"Yeah, I think it is." Ray comes next to me and helps me up.

No way this is over, it's just about to begin.

6

DESTRUCTION

Flashes of light blare through my dark room. I rub my tired eyes and get my bearings. The cell phone dances along the wooden nightstand, sending light beams all around. Ugh, who the hell is calling me at four in the morning? I pop up to a sitting position. Dear God, did someone die? I grab my phone and stare at the bright screen. Three missed calls from Ray.

I search for Ray's contact info and press the screen so hard it's a miracle it doesn't break. Please let Ray be okay. My hand trembles as I wait for him to answer.

"Lys."

The sound of his voice alive and well lifts a weight off of my shoulders.

"Yeah. What's wrong?" I doubt he'd be calling me this early to watch the sunrise.

He sighs. "I just got a call from the alarm company. Someone broke into the Kraken. I've just called the police and I'm headed up there."

You've got to be kidding me. This screams Jared. "Okay, I'll be right there."

I hang up the phone and click on the light. Maybe I'm jumping to conclusions. There were hundreds of people at the Kraken for the fights. Anyone could've come back and broken in. I huff. Who am I kidding?

I head to the bathroom and glance at myself in the mirror. Did a train run over me in my sleep? I wouldn't even go to the emergency room looking this bad. I slip on jean shorts and one of the Kraken t-shirts we had made, light makeup to cover up the dark circles under my eyes, and smack on some candy apple lip-gloss. A quick ponytail and I'm ready. For what exactly, is still to be determined.

The dark quiet night freaks me out. I guess I watched too many horror movies back in the day. Of course, it could be the one I lived out for five years. I scan the area and run to my car like Michael Myers is chasing me with a butcher knife. I slide into the seat and fire up the engine, checking the backseat to make sure it's empty before I drive off. One of my many little quirks. Who knows, maybe Ray will think they're cute.

The short ride to the Kraken goes by in a flash. A side effect of the combination of no traffic and my heavy foot. Two police cars sit in front of the entrance. I park and head inside.

Broken glass greets me as I walk through the front door. I gasp and look around at the damage. This was no break in. Someone deliberately trashed the place. Every bottle of liquor in the bar is smashed. The barstools are tossed across the restaurant floor. Huge slashes in the orange vinyl booths make them look like Freddy Kruger mauled them into pieces. Glass scatters across the floor. Even the ceiling fans are ripped off the ceiling and dismantled into pieces. Is anything here salvageable?

Ray stands across the room talking to Wade, the police chief. Also known as Jared's brother. My hands ball into fists as I march across the room.

I point my finger at him. "You better do your job and take care of this." I gesture around the room.

"I'm here doing just that." Wade smirks.

"You know exactly what I mean. This whole deal is Jared's doing." Heat flushes through my body. I clench my fists tighter, trying to suppress my urge to punch Wade in the face.

"Do you have any evidence of this, ma'am? The security cameras were damaged and the little footage we have just shows a figure in all black." He slides his pen behind his ear. "The perpetrator put Vaseline on the cameras. Can't see a damn thing." He slides his notebook into his pocket.

The fires of hell rip through me. Wade knows that whole Vaseline trick was concocted by Jared. He tried to disprove the theory when I was watching a show about paparazzi and a celebrity trick was to rub lip balm on the camera to prevent them from getting a good picture.

A shiny object across the room catches my attention. I squint, searching to identify it. No idea if it's a piece of metal from the destroyed dining room or other junk. I can't shake the feeling that I need to go check it out.

Wade's piercing voice fades away as I walk across the room and retrieve the object. My stomach drops to the floor. A silver dollar, Jared always carries one in his pocket. He thinks it brings him luck. I snatch it and hold it out in front of me, marching toward Wade and Ray.

"Who's to blame now, Wade?" I tap my foot and shoot him a death glare.

Wade's eyes widen for a split second before returning to their mischievous squint. "Must've fell out of someone's pocket at the fights."

He tries to take it from me put I yank it away. "Are you fucking kidding me? You know your asshole brother carries one of these around in his pocket." I charge toward him but Ray grabs me a few seconds before I reach him. "Jared thinks a silver dollar's going to change his shitty life. You can both go to hell."

Wade shakes his head. "Mr. Wilson, if you find anything else, please contact the sheriff's office. In the meantime, I'll write up the police report for your insurance company." He looks at me and tips his hat. "Ma'am."

I struggle to get away from Ray and pummel Wade but Ray's strong arms keep me from escaping. Once Wade is out of our field of vision Ray releases his grip.

"Maybe you should take up boxing."

I smile and shake off the hellfire flowing through me, but it all comes raging out. "Jared is behind this. I know it and he gets away with it…all of it because his family owns this godforsaken town. Why the hell would you come back here? All that's left is bad memories and aggravation." I cover my face with my hands and try to hold back the impending tears threatening to fall.

"I know things changed for the worse when I left. Between Rick's accident and all this political crap it's not the same. But it's still home." He walks over to me and tucks a stray hair behind my ear.

I drop my hands and look up at him, my eyes still welled with tears.

He lifts my chin and presses his forehead against mine. "Plus, I met you."

"You've known me forever."

"Not like this. And if everything didn't happen the way it did, I might not be back here. I might not be with you. Don't you get it? Being with you is worth all of this."

Tingles sweep from my head to my feet. My heart pounds against my chest. The best compliment of my life from the most amazing man I've ever met. How am I supposed resist that? I'm not.

All the doubt disappears from my brain, replaced by pure passion. I lunge at Ray, smacking my lips into his. He stands, stunned for a moment like he just got a left hook to the face. A split second later, he wraps his arms around me and lifts me. Glass scatters across the floor creating a unique melody against the tile as he walks.

I weave my hands into the hair on the back of his neck. He lets out a low moan and kicks opened the door to his office. I breathe fast and heavy. Closing the door with his foot, he sets me on the leather couch next to his desk, and then hovers above me.

I pull away for a second and stare into his blue eyes, which pierce my soul. I've never wanted anyone more than I want Ray in this moment. I grab at his black T-shirt, pulling it up and over his head as if it is on fire. He glides his fingers under my oversized Kraken T-shirt and slides it off in between kisses. Passion takes over and I grab at his jeans, ripping open the button and sliding my hands inside. He lets out a loud moan as I run my hands over everything I desire.

Where did this sexy siren come from? The last time I felt like this was at my prom and I'm pretty sure this time will last more than five minutes. Being with Jared was more like a job, one I couldn't wait to quit. But being with Ray, it's like I won the lottery ten times. He unhooks my bra and tosses it into oblivion, rubbing his calloused fingers over my breasts. I moan with pleasure. The sound ignites something in the both of us.

Ray pulls away and sits up. His sculpted body glistens in the low light in the room. He rips off my jean shorts in one swoop and hooks a finger on each side of my panties, pulling them down. He tucks them in his back pocket and stands up for a minute, sliding off his jeans and boxers. He pulls a condom from his wallet and slides it on in less than five seconds. His moves were always legendary but to see them in person is awe-inspiring. For once, the fabled tales are true.

He grabs my thighs and yanks me toward him, thrusting himself inside me. I let out a moan that I'm sure the whole street can hear the second he fills me. We move together, creating a rhythm that brings me to the brink of pleasure within a few minutes. I dig my fingers into his back as I release my desire. The world stands still. Energy created between us rivals that of the waves crashing into the sand. I suck in air, trying to catch my breath.

He buries his head into my shoulder, thrusting inside me slow and steady. I match his moves, to give him even an ounce of the pleasure he provides. Desire takes over and I wrap my legs around him, pushing him as deep inside me as possible. I moan, words I can barely comprehend coming out of my mouth. His heart pounds against my chest like it's going to escape and fly across the room. I squeeze my legs tighter and move in ways I didn't know I could. He throbs inside of me, letting out a loud moan before finding his release.

The heat of the moment spins me into a frenzy of desire and I find my pleasure again, right in time with his. We gasp to catch our breaths. He collapses on top of me. Every bit of energy we had we gave to each other. Exhausted and satisfied, a perfect way to feel.

I relax my thighs and he eases out of me. He lifts his head and presses his forehead against me, kissing my lips soft. I barely have the energy to reciprocate but I've never felt better. Is this the love that I read about in romance novels and decided was purely fiction and could never exist in reality? Hell yes. It's so real.

A knock resonates through the air, pulling me out of the afterglow. Ray jumps up and dives into his clothes. I admire the view until the fabric covers his sculpted body. "Be right back."

I leap from the couch and throw on my clothes the same way I did when I was making out with Chris Perry back in high school and my mom knocked on the bedroom door. Dear God, it's like I worked out for three days straight. I stand on wobbly legs and peek through the opening of the door.

"Mr. Wilson." Wade's voice stabs through me. "I've got that police report all ready for you. Thought you'd want it in a hurry."

"Thanks, I'll get right on it." Ray holds out his hand.

Wade shakes it. "Sounds like you already did." He walks away.

"What did you say?" Ray walks toward Wade but stops, letting him leave.

I high tail it out of Ray's office and give him a quick wave. "See you later. Got an appointment to show a house in an hour." I pick up the pace to a slow jog, passing Wade on my way.

Great, I put on quite a show for our sheriff. I bet he can't wait to tell Jared, and God knows what he's planning next. Being with me is ruining everything Ray is trying to build. He's everything I want and I'm nothing he needs. How can something so perfect be so wrong? I can't be Ray's demise.

7

REDEMPTION

My cell phone dances across my kitchen table. I don't need to look at the screen to know who's calling: it's Ray. I guess I don't have the guts to talk to him right now. I keep bailing out without any explanation. If a guy did that to me I'd be wrist deep in a gallon of chocolate marshmallow ice cream with a vodka chaser.

A chime catches my attention. Okay, he left a voicemail. He probably thinks I'm still at the house showing anyway… you know, the fictional one. Truth be told, business hasn't been booming in weeks. If Ray hadn't hired me, I don't know what I'd do.

I slide my hand across the table and grip the phone. Guess it's now or never. I hold it to my ear and press play. "Lys, I know what you're doing. Hell, I've done it enough times myself. Gotta say, it sucks on this end. Anyway, I'm coming over. We need to talk."

I drop the phone like I've just touched poison. Oh God,

I've got to leave before he gets here. No way in hell I can resist him if he's standing in front of me. Doesn't he get it? We're better off as friends just like we've always been.

I grab my keys and head toward the door, pulling it opened with the strength of Conan the Barbarian.

Ray leans against the doorjamb. I gaze at his perfectly messy hair, damp like he just got out of the shower. Those baby blues pierce through me and I know there's no hope for me. I let out the breath I'd been holding.

"Hot date?" He flashes a smile.

I open my mouth to speak but nothing comes out.

He holds a finger over my lips. "Please just hear me out."

I nod. It's not like I can do anything else. I'm completely powerless, captivated by his charm.

"I get it. You're scared. But I'm not that asshole you married. You know me, Lys. You know more about me than any girl I've ever been with my whole life." He tucks a stray hair behind my ear. "You've seen me at my best, at my worst, and everywhere in between. And I've never been better than when I'm with you." He drops his finger from my lips.

I melt into a puddle. It takes every ounce of my being to refrain from jumping into his arms and riding off into the sunset.

"Ray...everything is different now."

"Exactly." He presses his forehead against mine.

I take a step back. I sure as hell can't think when he's this close to me. "Listen, you're starting over, and being with me is ruining it all for you." I nibble my lip.

He scrunches his eyebrows. "Not true, Lys."

"Come on, Ray. If we weren't working together or whatever we're doing, you'd..."

"I'd be sunk. You got the Kraken noticed, marketed, managed. Sure, there's a few snags but without you, I'd be dead in the water. Try again."

I'm sure he'd find someone else to do all the things I've done to help launch his business but I'll play his game.

"From the minute you saw me, you wanted to save me. I'm fine. I get it, you're trying to make up for not being there for Rick by becoming my white knight." Oh God, please tell me I didn't say that out loud.

Ray gasps like he's just been sucker punched. His eyes well with tears but he blinks before any can fall.

I'm a bigger asshole than Jared. Ray has this guilt from Rick's death which he couldn't stop whether he was in town or not and I just poured salt in that wound. What the hell is wrong with me? I sure as hell don't deserve him and he'll never want to be with me now. I guess I did what I wanted. I pushed him away. A few tears fall down my cheeks, I quickly wipe them away. I walk toward him and rest a hand on his shoulder. "I'm sorry, I didn't mean it."

He nods. "Yes you did, and you're right...at first." He blows air out of puffed cheeks. "But after I saw you swinging at the sheriff, I know you can take care of yourself." He lifts my chin. "Try again, hit me with your best shot."

Really? He still wants to be with me after that? He's clearly insane. I shrug. "I got nothing."

"Lys." He stares into my eyes. "Look me in the eye and tell me you don't feel the same way."

I swallow hard. "I can't."

"Exactly." He presses his lips against mine sucking my bottom lip. "Hot date tonight at seven. Don't run this time." He winks and walks out the door, closing it behind him.

I stand, frozen. I think he knows me better than I know myself. Dammit!

Beep Beep. The loud horn blares through the air, almost causing me to smudge the finishing touches of my lipstick. I pull the curtain to the side. Ray slings an arm over the leather seat, kind of the way guys do when they want to put their arm around a girl in the movie theater. He looks toward my front door.

I slip on my flip flops and take one last glance at my hair. I adjust the elastic band holding my hair in a loose ponytail. Eh, the top is down on his convertible so I'll hope for sexy messy. I hop down the steps and grab my purse on the way out the door. Wait, he did say this was a date. Why isn't he coming to the door?

A sexy smile graces Ray's face as I walk toward him. A gust of wind blows my sundress in too many directions to count. Great, now the neighbors have seen my new purple underwear. Guess I should've gone the casual route but it's been so many years since I've been on a real date. For the first time in forever, I wanted to put on a dress and do up my make-up. Best I've felt about myself in I can't remember how long.

Ray slides off his sunglasses, dangling them over the steering wheel. He looks me up and down from head to toe.

"God, you're gorgeous." He leans over and opens the passenger side door for me. "Your chariot awaits."

I bite my lip, to suppress the ear-to-ear smile about to burst out. "Thanks. You look pretty good yourself." I slide into the leather seat and pat down my dress. "Did you want to come in first?"

He shakes his head. "We're kicking it old school tonight… you know, like we did back in the day."

I can't help staring at his dark blue shirt, clinging to his muscles in just the perfect way. The way they move resembles a mating dance. I continue to glance down at his charcoal gray board shorts. Dear God, I bet he could even make Speedos look good.

He turns on the radio, pulling me back into reality. "Work your magic."

I move the dial to my go to classic rock channel. *Home Sweet Home* by Mötley Crüe blasts through the airwaves. Somehow it's the most appropriate song that could play for our so-called date.

"Nice." He slides on his sunglasses and drives down the road.

"Back in the day guys came up to my door when we going on a date. Did women just throw themselves into your car?"

He turns toward me and then looks back at the road. "They did call the car a chick magnet." He nudges me. "Come on, Lys. You know how it was back in the day. Jump in the car and drive off. Let the wind be our guide."

"Did you join the Hell's Angels or something?"

He flashes a quick smile. "Nah, couldn't trade the 'Vette

for a bike." He turns onto the coastal highway. "Close your eyes."

Is he serious? "Why. Did you and Rick build a secret highway I never knew about?"

"I'll never tell." He glances over at me and then back toward the road. "Come on."

"Fine, but you better not close yours too." I fold my arms across my chest and close my eyes. What the hell is he doing? I've been here my whole life. There's nothing he can show me I haven't already seen. No surprises here.

"Okay, now when you open them, pretend it's ten years ago. No responsibility, no baggage, just me and you." An involuntary smile graces my face. If only it was that easy.

"Open them."

I open my eyes and look over toward Ray. A smile spreads across my face like wildfire. I hold my hands up in the air and lift my head, letting the air dance across my body. The weight lifts off of my chest as if I'm in an outer space no gravity zone. "Woo hoo!" It leaves my mouth like it used to when I rode in a convertible back in the day.

Ray lifts his arm like Judd Nelson in the *Breakfast Club*. "I should've taken you out back then but I was way too stupid."

"Don't you think Rick would've been pissed?" I raise my eyebrows.

He shakes his head. "Not if he knew the way I felt…but then again I didn't know it back then either, but I do now."

Chills sweep through me. He slides his arm down and intertwines his fingers with mine. A kaleidoscope of butterflies flow through my body. My heart rate doubles the second his skin touches mine. Every cell in my body knows just what Ray can do to me. Did the temperature just rise?

We turn the corner and Ray pulls over to an old building.

I squint, struggling to read the tattered sign. "Oh my God, that used to be the Sailor's Shack." Besides the Kraken, the Sailor's Shack was our other hangout. It's at the bottom of the coast by the bridge. Once you cross it you're at Turtle Bay, the next town over. Sailor's Shack had the best milkshakes on the eastern seaboard. I heard the owners shut down and went to live in Florida a few years back. "You know this place is closed, right?"

He shuts down the car. "Guess I better improvise, then." He walks over and opens the door for me. "Better date etiquette?" He holds out his hand.

I take his hand and step out of the car. "Much." Truth be told, I don't care if he says all the right things or opens doors for me. The way I feel when we're together makes up for all the small stuff. Who am I kidding? Ray is always a gentleman. He's trying to delve into the past. Acting like he did when we were young. Maybe he's creating a redo.

I walk up the sandy path that's scattered with pieces of seashells until I reach the building that used to be Sailor's Shack. Tattered paint chips speckle the sand and withered wood makes it look like it's been through the brunt of a thousand storms. What are we doing here?

"Are we having a picnic?" I peek through an opening in the door.

He grabs the handle. "Nope, I'm taking you out to Sailor's Shack, like I should've done ten years ago." He pulls opened the door.

I cover my mouth with my hands. Strings of Christmas lights and dangling wooden anchors hang from the ceiling, draping down the corners of the room. A table, complete with a white linen tablecloth and a candle burning in the center, sits in the middle of the room.

A woman wearing a black dress smiles and gestures toward the table. "Wilson, party of two. Right this way."

Ray places his hand in the small of my back and guides me to the table. He pulls out a chair.

Wait, she's Sabrina, the new bartender at the Kraken. I sit down and gaze around. Okay, nothing looks like it did back in the day. Sailor's Shack was a teenager hangout. There was an arcade Pac-man game in the corner, a surfboard hanging from the wall, nets with starfish in every corner, and lots of slang sailor sayings framed and hanging from the wall.

"I thought we'd class up the joint a little. You know… evolve over time, just like us, Lys." Ray gestures for the woman to come over to our table.

My heart flutters in my chest. No one has ever hired a waitress, chef, and God knows who else, to pull off the perfect date for me. Tingles sweep through my body from my head to my toes.

Hell, Jared proposed to me half-drunk on the beach. No dinner, no planning, nothing special. I guess that's when my self-esteem hit rock bottom. Doesn't matter. That's ancient history.

Who knew Prince Charming would ride in with a blue corvette and boxing gloves. I flash the smile I can no longer hold in. How did I get so lucky to win his heart?

The waitress comes over with two menus. I take one and

Ray takes the other. I peruse the entrees and snicker. It's the classic Sailor Shack menu. Milkshakes, sandwiches, nachos… it's all there just the same as when we were teenagers.

"Can't mess with perfection." Ray winks.

"You're crazy." I let out a laugh. "Totally awesomely insane."

He leans across the table. "Crazy about you."

I lean toward him. "Ditto." I press my lips against his, striving to suppress my urge to tackle him to the floor and have my way with him. "Just so you, this is the best date of my life."

"I was just trying to get you to agree to a second date." He presses his forehead against mine.

"How about I reserve a third and fourth one?" I kiss him again, sucking on his bottom lip as I pull away.

"I like the way you think."

The waitress clears her throat.

I take the hint and sit back in my chair. "I'll have a vanilla shake, the loaded sailor burger and cheese fries."

"Same for me." Ray places my menu underneath his and hands them to the waitress. "I hired the original chef. He works at the new hotel down the road put I managed to strike a deal with him so he'd call off."

"You're full of surprises Mr. Wilson." I drape my napkin over my lap.

"I'm just getting started."

"Good, me too."

A snap resonates through the air like someone stepped on a twig in the forest. Ray looks up at the ceiling the second on of the decorative wooden anchors come crashing down. It hits him directly in his eye. He blinks repeatedly and then jumps up from the table. He steps back, knocking over his chair and waving his hands in front of him like he's running from a serial killer in the pitch dark.

I spring into action and rush to his side. "Ray…are you okay?"

He shakes his head like he's just taken a hit from Mike Tyson and is trying to regain focus. He holds his hand over his eye. I grab his shoulder but he yanks it away. What is happening?

I lean over toward his ear, still trying to keep as much distance as I can. "Ray, it's Lys."

He stops and lets his muscles relax. He takes a deep breath and slowly exhales. "I'm fine." He takes his hand away from his eye. "Just having a little trouble seeing. You know, like when you get sunscreen in your eye. Same feeling."

I rush over to him and turn his chin toward mine. "Let me see." I run my hand along his cheek and examine his eye. It's completely red, like blood took over the white of his eye. "I think we should head to the hospital."

He shakes his head. "Nah, just a boxing injury. It'll be fine by tomorrow." He picks up the anchor. "Guess I should've gotten the plastic ones." He slings an arm around me. "Our food is probably almost ready." He walks me back to my seat and then picks his chair up from the floor, sitting down at the table like nothing happened.

My hands tremble. Great, a flashback from my past. Ray would never hurt me, I know that but the way he just acted was like…he was a wounded animal. I guess this is the injury that caused him to retire. Maybe getting hit like that puts him right back in the ring, ready to fight for survival. I know the feeling well.

The waitress brings over our milkshakes. Mine would be better with a little rum in it at the moment. I take a sip and let the sweet concoction take over my senses. No reason to let one mishap ruin this amazing date. The vanilla shake takes me right back to carefree days of living for the moment. It's exactly the same, perfect.

"What's next for the Kraken?" I bite my burger the second the waitress sets it in front of me.

"Hmm, let me ask my marketing director." He scarfs down his burger in three bites. Some things never change.

I drag a fry through some cheese and pop it in my mouth. "Once, we're back to pristine condition. I was thinking we could lie low for a little while, make sure all the smoke clears and plan a big Halloween Bash. It'll be here sooner than you think."

Ray raises his eyebrows and nods. "I don't know how you do it." He shoves a bunch of fries in his mouth. "Great idea. Maybe we could do a haunted shipwreck theme."

"That's amazing. Are you sure you need me around?" I slug down the rest of my shake.

"Oh yeah. It's pretty much the only thing I'm sure of right now."

Chills sweep through me and they have nothing to do with the cold milkshake. How does he do it? He makes me feel like I'm sixteen again and anything can happen, like the world is my oyster.

He waves over to the waitress. "Wanna split?"

"Sure." I reach for my purse.

Ray puts his hand down on top of mine. "Come on, Lys. Don't you remember?"

The waitress comes over with a boat, filled with ice cream, chocolate sauce, whipped cream, and a slew of fruit.

How the hell could I forget about the famous Sailor's Split? Rick and Ray downed one each homecoming weekend while a crowd of football players and cheerleaders applauded. The owner's even gave them free T-shirts.

"Okay, I know Rick and I have the same DNA, but there's no way I can eat that."

"I'll share this time." He chuckles and hands me a spoon. "Dig in, it's like eating heaven."

A lot of things resemble heaven when I'm with Ray. I take an oversized spoonful of the sundae and eat it. Whipped cream and chocolate drips along my lips, I must be a mess.

Ray leans forward. He cups my chin with his hand and kisses my lip. "Did I ever tell you how sweet you taste?"

My heart rate triples. "First time I'm ever hearing it."

"Then I should say it more." He kisses me again, increasing in passion.

I let out a low moan. Wait, there's another person in here. I pull away and sit back. "Can't let our split melt." It's amazing it's not boiling from the heat generated between the two of us.

He leans back in his seat and glances over toward the waitress. "Right." He takes a whole scoop of ice cream in one spoonful. "Better eat it quick." He winks.

Subtle. I laugh and shovel some more of the sundae in my mouth. I haven't had anything like this in years. Watching what I ate, working out all the time, and depriving myself of the things I love. What was I thinking? Everything in moderation is the key and that's my new mantra. Except for Ray, I need to indulge in him every chance I get.

We finish the sundae in record speed, mostly thanks to Ray. He pulls out his chair and comes over to me, holding out his hand. I take it and stand up. What is he up to now? Please let it be something private.

He waves to the waitress and guides me out of the reinvented Sailor's Shack and out to the beach. The cool moonlight radiates my skin as it hangs over the waves, crashing onto the sand. I breathe deep, taking in the salty air. If I could concoct a perfect date with Ray in my head, it wouldn't be close to as good as this one. I squeeze his hand to just make sure this isn't a dream.

We walk to a blanket set up in the sand next to a fire pit. A cooler sits next to the blanket. He guides me over and we both sit down.

"Beach party for two." He opens the cooler and hands me a wine cooler. "Fuzzy naval still your favorite?"

I nod. How the hell does he remember? I twist open the cap and take a slug.

He pulls out his cell phone and starts one of his playlists. He shows me the screen. *Rick and Ray's classics.*

"Perfect." And I don't just mean the music choice.

I Was Made for Loving You by KISS flows through the air. I nuzzle up to Ray, resting my head on his shoulder. He leans back, guiding me down until we're both lying on the blanket staring up at the stars. Other than the mishap with Ray's eye, this night couldn't be more amazing if I concocted it in one of my daydreams. For once, reality is better. I turn toward Ray and get lost in the moment, nothing else exists and I want to stay here forever.

He props himself on an elbow and tips my chin up. My heart pounds, beating faster the closer his lips come to mine. I wrap my arms around him, weaving my fingers in his hair. He feathers his fingers along my breasts, down to the hem of my dress, slowly feathering them up my thigh.

I let out a low moan as he continues his journey, sliding my underwear to the side and pressing his fingers inside me. I breathe heavy and deep. We're on the beach, what if someone comes over?

"Ray," I mutter in between breaths but I suddenly can't remember what it is I wanted to say. I slide my hands down to his jeans and unbutton them, sticking my hand inside and holding all I desire.

He pulls out his wallet, grabbing a condom, and rips it open with his teeth. I take it from him and slide it on like my mom's about to come home and I'm short on time. He pulls down my underwear and thrusts inside me. I let out a moan that I'm sure they heard back at the Sailor's Shack and grab a hold of him, wrapping my legs around him tight.

He moves slow and steady, the passion growing between us. Electric shocks pulse along my body every time he thrusts inside of me. I breathe so heavy it's like I'm gasping for air. No other man in the world even comes close to Ray. It's like he has a personal roadmap of my body and knows exactly what to do and when to do it. I dig my fingers through his T-shirt into his back as I find my release.

The passion runs through my blood. I roll Ray over and straddle him desperate to give him the pleasure he gives to me.

I'm never one of those take charge kind of girls in the bedroom but Ray turns on the sexy siren inside. I rock back and forth, pressing myself against him.

He mutters some words I can't translate and grabs my hips, moving them in rhythm with his. He lets out a moan and grabs me tight as he releases his passion. The built-up desire inside me bursts at the same time. I breathe heavy and collapse on top of him.

We get our bearings straight for a moment and I roll over, easing him out of me. I lie on the blanket, catching my breath and reliving the last twenty minutes of pleasure in my mind.

Ray props up on a shoulder and turns toward me. "Best date ever."

I let out a chuckle and playfully slap him. Ray can bring me back to that high school girl in a second flat. I love that about him. Nothing needs to be overanalyzed; we don't need to worry about what happens next. It's just us, like it's always been.

"Most fun I've ever had with my dress still on." I find my underwear thrown on top of the cooler and slide them on.

"Hmm, sounds like a challenge." He zips up his pants and winks.

I look around the deserted beach. It looks like no one caught us, not that I really care. Even if they did, it was so worth it.

A few drops of rain fall onto my face. I wipe them off and stand up. "I think we're getting rained out."

"Huh, guess that 20% chance of rain is happening." He hops up and grabs his phone and the cooler, sticking our empty bottles inside.

I grab the blanket and fold it up. The rain starts pouring down. Ray takes my hand. We run toward the parking lot. A smile creeps across my face. It's that whole carefree persona I have when I'm with Ray. I feel the way I used to before the Jared days…happy.

We toss the blanket and cooler in the back seat. Ray puts up the top. He leans in, wiping down the leather seats quick before we jump inside. He fires up the engine and pulls out of the parking lot.

He runs a hand through his hair. "Didn't want the date to end yet."

I readjust my wet hair into the ponytail. "Who said it has to end?"

He looks over at me and nods, a smile gracing his face. "Where to, my lady?" He looks back at the road.

"I guess you should take me home."

He lowers his eyebrows. "I thought you didn't want the date to end."

"I don't." I put my hand on his thigh. "Stay."

He presses the pedal and revs the engine. Time for Round Two.

8
CHALLENGES

A RIPPLE OF WHITE SATIN FLOWS ACROSS MY SHEETS. I TURN and gaze at the perfect specimen of the male anatomy lying next to me. The sleek fabric drapes over his waist, the muscles of his arms and torso exposed and gleaming in the sunlight. Dear God, please imprint this image on my brain for all of eternity.

Ray stretches and turns toward me. "So, are you a coffee first kind of girl?"

Is he insane? After the amazing date last night? Hell no, he perks me up more than a million cups of coffee. I lunge over on top of him, smacking my lips against his. He holds me in his arms. My heart races the second his skin touches mine.

The theme from Rocky blasts through the room, pulling me out of the seductress zone. Ray's muscles relax and he almost throws me off of him to grab the phone.

"Sorry Lys, it's my manager, Dennis." He grabs the phone. "Hello."

Really? The theme from Rocky. Is he going to be calling me Adrian later?

He jumps out of bed. "Wait. Are you serious?"

I stare at the muscles of his butt, dancing underneath his boxers. Remind me to thank his manager later for the view.

"Yeah, let's do it."

He shuts off the phone and puts his hands on his head. He lowers them and turns toward me. The look on his face mocks that of a lottery winner.

"Lys, you're not going to believe this. Dennis set up a fight."

A chill blasts down my spine. "Like for charity or something?" I get that boxing is his passion but he retired for a reason.

He paces around the room, a smile beaming from his face. "It's exhibition but a real fight. I'm coming out of retirement for a one-night-only event. Me and Tommy "Tommy Gun" Lewoski." He jumps on the bed and kneels in front of me. "Can you believe it, Lys?"

The blood drains from my face. Not really. Is he crazy? I saw what happened at Sailor's Shack and that was a small piece of wood. What's going to happen if Tommy hits him in the eye? Is one fight worth going blind…or worse.

"Come on, Lys. You're looking at me like I just ate the last piece of chocolate cake in the history of the world." He pulls me toward him into a hug. "The Wrecker is back." He releases his hold.

It's like his brain erased the last few years. He didn't even mention his injury to his manager or any precautions that might be taken. He just screamed YES! like the love of his life proposed to him at Disney World. Do I seriously have to piss in his Cheerios and be the voice of reason?

"I'm just worried. You know, about your eye." I wipe a few stray hairs from his forehead and run my hand down his cheek. "You retired for a reason, right?"

He sighs. "I can handle it." He gets out of bed and puts on his jeans. "I'm not a washed-up has-been. I can still fight. They'll see."

Where the hell did that come from? "I know you can. But it might be a good idea to check in with the doctor and let them know about the fight. Maybe you'll have to adjust your game."

He looks up at me and nods. "Good point. I'll call her and make an appointment." He kisses me on the cheek. "Always looking out for me." He winks. "I gotta go call my trainer and get things set up. Fight night is in a month. Not a ton of time." He runs out the door like the building is on fire.

What the hell just happened?

Ray's knee bounces, his foot tapping the floor at warp speed. I put my hand on his leg, trying to calm his nerves. God knows what he told Dr. Kline to get an appointment three hours after he called. I insisted on being here with him, even though he probably doesn't want me to hear what she has to say. Who knows, maybe she'll surprise me.

I look around the waiting room. Miss Fritz, our second grade teacher, sits in a chair at the far side of the room reading People magazine. She looks over at us every so often and squints, trying to place us. Let's hope she doesn't remember when Ray and Rick filled her desk with plastic snakes. She jumped so far she tripped over the chair and sprained her ankle.

The only other person in the waiting room is Mr. Clancy, who owns Seaside Books. He waved to us when we came in but he's more of a reader than a talker. He's nose-deep in the new Stephen King novel as he waits for the doctor.

The door opens and butterflies fill my stomach. What's going on? I'm not the one who should be nervous. This is my last hoorah to get Ray to decline the fight offer. Truth be told, I doubt he'll change his mind no matter what she's says, but this is my last hope.

"Ray...come on in." I hop up from the chair and practically drag Ray into the office.

He takes a seat on the table.

The nurse, Rebecca Fenster, is practically screwing Ray with her eyes. I guess she forgot he never looked twice at her back in the day, and he sure as hell isn't going to now. I take a deep breath and slowly exhale. Okay, maybe I'm a little on edge. Women ogling Ray is nothing new, and I'm not the jealous type. I've got to relax.

Dr. Kline comes into the room and sets down her chart. "Ray, it's great to see you."

"You too, Doc."

"What brings you in? You said it was an emergency." She gives him a once-over.

Really? Emergency? It's like he's lost his mind. Maybe I should have made an appointment with the psychiatrist instead.

"I got a fight offer. Me and 'Tommy Gun' Lewoski in a month. I've got this problem with my eye and I wanted you to take a look at it." He nibbles his lip.

She pulls up a chair and sits down next to Ray. "I looked at your chart, Ray. You had a retinal hemorrhage and detachment. It happens to a lot of boxers. Our bodies aren't made to get hit repeatedly. The trauma over the years has caused damage to your retina. If you keep getting hit in your left eye you can go blind permanently." She sighs. "I wish I had better news. If you get hit hard enough during the fight you'll lose your vision in your left eye, temporarily or maybe permanently, and even though I'm not a boxer I think you'll need to see out of both of them. I can't recommend you go through with it."

Ray blows out of puffed cheeks. "So, if I don't get hit I should be fine."

Did he seriously just say that? It's like talking to a wall. Everything he hears he twists around to make it something he wants to hear.

"Thank you, Dr. Kline." I stand up and try to control the raging fire inside. Ugh, I just want to shake some sense into him. I've got to talk to him, or I'll regret it.

"See ya later, Doc. Thanks for the advice." He shakes Dr. Kline's hand and we head out of the office.

I stomp to the car and plop inside. What is he thinking? He retired for a reason and bought the Kraken, which is sitting in shambles at the moment. It's like he's trying to chase a past that doesn't exist anymore. One that might get him seriously hurt…or worse.

He slides in the car and closes the door. He turns toward

me. "Look, I know what you're going to say. It's dangerous and I shouldn't do it. But I need this."

I shift my weight to face him and throw my hands in the air. "One phone call and you're ready to bail on everything here? Just pick up and leave for a month to box one more time?" I shake my head. "Are you planning on leaving me with the mess?"

He puts his hand on my knee. "Lys, no. I'll take care of everything."

I push his hand away and press my lips in a flat line. "How? The Kraken just opened. You can't close a business for a month and then reopen it when you feel like working. You made a commitment and now you're taking off."

He takes a deep breath. "The Kraken is being repaired. I know you worked hard to market it and I'm sorry. I've got to do this. I need one more shot to prove myself."

I shrug. "For what? To lose everything you built here?"

He shakes his head. "You'll never understand." He covers his face with his hands and drags them down his chin. "Once I get this last fight, I'm done. I need one last chance and then I'll be able to walk away on my terms."

I roll my eyes. "You're right I don't understand. I don't get why you can't just leave it behind you and stick with the fresh start you made here…with the Kraken…with me."

He tips my chin toward him. "This has nothing to do with me and you."

I look down and turn away. "Please take me home."

He pauses for a minute and fires up the engine, slowly pulling onto the road.

Doesn't he get it? It has everything to do with us. He's

zipping away like a bat out of hell and leaving everything here in limbo. He has responsibilities and he's just taking off and flying by the seat of his pants.

Ugh, it's like a Jared flashback. He always jumped from one job to another, never fully committing himself to anything, and I had to pick up the pieces. I finally got away from all of that and started my own business, which has been suffering because I've been working on the Kraken, and for what? I can't keep following the same path.

Ray pulls up in front of my house. He shuts down the engine. "Lys, I leave tonight to train."

Dear God, it's only been a few hours since the phone call. My cousin didn't leave this soon when she found out she was getting a kidney transplant.

"You gotta do what you gotta do, right?" I reach for the door handle.

Ray grabs my arm. "I can't leave like this, Lys."

I shake off his arm. "What do you want from me, Ray? You want me to tell you this is great. You want me to watch you ruin everything you worked for since you got here? It's not happening. I'm out."

I step out of the car and slam the door, bolting into the house. The engine roars and Ray speeds off. What did I just do?

Three weeks and nothing, no phone calls, texts, emails just complete silence. Every boxing movie I've ever watched have the same thing in common, no significant other issues while training. Your head is supposed to be clear so you only concentrate on the fight. I guess I screwed that rule up, big time. Even though every shred of my being wants to run to Ray, I need to stay away from him or things can get worse. My heart's been shattered before but right now it's pulverized. No matter what, I can't talk to him, not yet.

I did make a commitment to the Kraken and I'm still Ray's employee so I'm going to try to save it from floating away into the sea of closed down businesses. I push open the door to Joe's Hardware and search for some items to make a sign for the door. Might as well let this fight do some good for Ray. A Fight Night Pay-Per-View showing could boost business, especially since the owner is in the ring. I'll get the Kraken spruced up and ready to go.

The voice that makes my skin crawl floats through the air. What the hell is Jared doing here? He's literally the last person I need to see right now. I duck behind an aisle to avoid him.

"Hey, I hear Tommy's fighting Ray. You heading to Vegas?" Joe says to Jared.

I scrunch my eyebrows. Jared's never been into boxing. What the hell is going on?

"Nah, I'll watch it on Pay-Per-View. Better view from my living room anyway. I'm sure my cuz will kick ass, just like he always does." Jared's boots stomp across the floor. "See ya, Joe." He walks out of the store.

What is he talking about? Memories of our wedding run through my mind like a freight train. His cousin Tommy. My God, he's "Tommy Gun", the boxer. Son of a bitch, did Jared have something to do with this fight? Heat engulfs my face.

9

WRATH

Atomic fury runs through my veins. I press my lips together holding in the primal screams about to come out. Satan himself isn't this soulless of a creature. I suck in a deep breath and slowly exhale, returning my blood pressure to an acceptable level.

"Alyssa, do you need help?" Joe calls to me from the end of the aisle.

Yes, I may need to cover up a murder. "Just grabbing a few things. I'll meet you at the register." I don't even turn around to look at him. I'd probably either burst into flames or tears.

I clutch the items I need and head to the checkout. Thank God I'm the master of fake smiles from all the shit that Jared put me through over the years. I slap one of my signature "everything's fine" smiles on and hold out my credit card.

Joe scrunches his eyebrows and searches my face. "You okay? Your face is red as a beet."

I nod. "A little too much sun." Jared has also perfected my

skill of making excuses. At least this time it's not an overabundance of make-up to cover up a bruise. I pay for the items and rush out of the store. "Thanks, Joe."

I plop my bag on the passenger seat of my car and fire up the engine. Blood rushes through my veins at warp speed. If the zombie apocalypse was upon us I think I'd be more relaxed. I've got one last shot at stopping Ray. Only thing, it might destroy me. I press the pedal and head to the one place I swore I'd never step foot again.

I pull to the side of the road and stare at the white colonial house with the red shutters that was my prison for five years. My hands shake the second I shut off the engine. I take a deep breath and banish all the dark memories trying to surface. A wave of nausea plunges through me. Why do I feel like I'm about to sell my soul to the devil?

Jared's probably stealthier than Satan. He plays on your hopes and dreams to destroy you. All Ray wants is to be what he once was, a champion. Little does he know this rigged fight is intended on hurting him…or worse. And all of it is because he's with me. Must be a hell of a payoff for Tommy to be sucked into Jared's plan.

I sigh. Telling Ray that Jared is behind this fight will only make him want to win more. Plus, it would make the whole deal so much more than defeating Tommy. I know Ray; he'd see a victory as proving himself worthy, beating Jared, and saving me. He's always played the role of the White Knight saving the damsel in distress. How can I stop him from walking into the lion's den?

I nibble at my nails. There's no other way. The only chance I have of saving Ray is to beg the devil himself to stop what he's doing and call it off, no matter what he makes me do in return.

I stare at the driveway, waiting for the bright red pick-up truck to pull in. So many times I've stared out the window doing this exact same thing. Back then, I was hoping he'd avoid killing anyone on the drive home and that he'd be so drunk he'd pass out in the garage until the next morning. It was rarely the case. He'd stagger in, knocking into the end table in the living room. After he broke two lamps, I learned to keep only shatter-proof items on the table. I'd scurry up to the bedroom and pretend I was sleeping until he came in and passed out. What is the sense in trying to talk to him in that condition? No one can reason with someone three sheets to the wind. I learned that the hard way. Who knows if I can reason with him sober, especially now?

The roar of the engine breaks through the silence in the car. My heart pounds louder the closer the truck comes to me. I take a deep breath and try to steady my trembling hands. He's here.

Jared pulls into the driveway and slams the car in park. He jumps out of the truck and tilts his head to the side, looking in my direction. Please, I'm sure he spotted me the second he drove down the road. He's playing with me, like a predator with his prey.

Is this what Ray feels like before he's about to step into the ring? Ready for battle, not sure if you're going to win or lose but you know damn well you're in for the fight of your life. You might get pummeled but you're going to give it all you've got.

I close my eyes for a second and focus. Come on, Alyssa you can do this. You battled him once before; sure it was in court with a lawyer but you still prevailed. He doesn't rule you anymore.

Jared makes a visor with his hand and walks in my direction. I take one last deep breath and get out of the car. Okay, it's go-time.

I close the door behind me and stand next to my car. No reason to move any closer. Besides it's probably best to stay off the property and he'll come to me.

"Lys…to what do I owe this pleasure?" He walks up to me, drops his hand to his side, and looks me up and down.

I clear my throat and swallow hard. "I was hoping we could talk."

"Talk?" He lets out a chuckle. "Now, didn't you say you'd never step foot here again and you wouldn't speak to me again if I was the last human being on earth?" He puts his finger to his lips and then looks around. "As far as I can see, the world hasn't ended."

What the hell was I thinking? Did I think the most arrogant asshole in the world was going to change? If only an asteroid would fly down from the heavens and incinerate him in the next few seconds. The world would be a better place.

I throw on a fake smile like I have for years. He wants a fight, but the only hope I have is to kill him with kindness. I've got to suck it up if I want to save Ray.

"I was harsh. Tempers were flying. Can we call a truce?" I

hold out my hand to shake his, trying to stop any trembling he might notice.

He scrunches his eyebrows. "I'm not an idiot, Lys."

I drop my hand down. Not entirely true.

"I know why you're here." He pops a cigarette in his mouth and lights it, blowing smoke in my face. "It's a done deal."

I cough and wave my hand in front of me to clear the air. "I know you, Jared. You've always got a price. What's it going to take to stop this fight?"

He shrugs. "I guess your boy can quit."

I ball my hand into a fist. It takes every ounce of energy to prevent myself from punching him in the face. Not that it would fare out well for me but it might be worth it this time. "You and Tommy cooked up this whole fight plan…for what? To hurt me? Well, mission accomplished."

He lets out a chuckle, a bellow of smoke pours out of his mouth. "Hate to inform you but the world doesn't revolve around you." He points his finger at me. "I have better things to do than think of ways to make poor Alyssa sad."

Ugh, his smug tone sends thunderbolts through my body. I bite the inside of my cheek for a few seconds to prevent any words from spewing out. If he's not trying to hurt me, which he is no matter what he says, what's this all about? A fight with Ray over who's a tougher man? Well, if Jared was doing the fighting and not hiding behind his cousin that theory would make more sense.

I fold my arms across my chest. "Okay, then why cook up this fight, Ray? What's in it for you?"

He takes a long drag of his cigarette and tosses the butt

into the road. "I've got quite a bit of cash riding on this deal. Someone took half of everything I own, plus I had to buy you out of the house. Oh, and lawyer bills. You know how it is, Lys." He shrugs. "Tearing you to pieces is just an added bonus." He smirks.

A primal scream erupts in my head. Jared's family has more money than God. He never paid for a blessed thing in his life. There's no way in hell he rigged this fight for cash. It's no use, he's not going to admit his motive even though it's clear he wants to run Ray out of town and destroy any happiness that comes my way.

I think back to the miserable days in my life when we were married. Groveling made him feel powerful and begging… well, that's the only way he'd stop. I have to be that girl one more time, the girl I thought I killed off the day I left. The girl I hate.

I let my arms fall to my sides and I walk up to him. The scent of stale cigarettes fills the space between us. My mind goes back to the day he came home drunk after losing a pool game to his brother. He started throwing whatever he could find across the room. When he grabbed the KISS record Rick gave me for my fifteenth birthday, my heart dropped to the floor. I ran up to Jared and dropped to my knees, holding onto him and begging him to give it back to me. Once he saw the power he had over me, he dropped to his knees and placed the record on the floor.

I take his hand, my eyes welling with tears. "Ray is the last shred of my brother that still exists. I can get you cash, whatever you want. I'll do whatever you want me to. Just please, call this off. What do I need to do to get you to stop this? I'll do anything." A stray tear rolls down my face.

He takes a finger and wipes it away. "You know I can't stand it when you cry. Even now." He lifts my chin. He stares into my eyes and takes a step back, yanking his hand away from me. "Five years...that's how long we were married. Never once have you defended me or stood up for me...and here you are begging me to stop this fight so your new boyfriend doesn't get hurt." He shakes his head and paces back and forth. "Not going to happen, Lys. You can get your ass back in your car and drive the hell away from here. There's nothing you can do to stop this fight. Ray is going to get destroyed and there's not a damn thing you can do about it." Jared storms off into the house and slams the door.

I let out the breath I didn't realize I was holding and burst into tears. I cover my face with my hands for a few seconds and then wipe them away as quick as I can. Stop it, Lys. You don't waste any more tears on him...ever. I swallow hard and compose myself on the short walk to my car. I fire up the engine and speed away, leaving Jared far behind me.

I pull into my driveway and rest my head on the steering wheel. What was I thinking? Jared would never do anything I ask, even if I could come up with a way to make it worth his while. He'd probably give up a million dollars just to see my life fall to shambles.

Desperation makes you do things you'd never dream of doing otherwise. Doesn't matter, I had to try. Jesus Christ, I made a hell of a mess out of this. Ray and I haven't spoken since I flipped out on him, selling my soul to the devil didn't work out the way I'd hoped, and this rigged fight can destroy everything. Am I in hell?

Detroit Rock City blasts through the air. I lift my head and turn toward the sweet music spewing from my purse. I dig in it at warp speed and grab my phone. The screen lights up the letters I've longed to see. Maybe the angels do have my back.

10

THE BATTLE

BEST RING TONE EVER. THE FAVORITE SONG OF THE TWO MEN I love most in life, Rick and Ray. I laugh and cry at the same time. I take a deep breath and slowly exhale. My trembling finger slides across the screen to answer.

"Hello." My heart pounds against my chest so fast it's amazing he can't hear it through the phone.

He takes a breath. "Sabrina called me. She's stoked for this Fight Night two event at the Kraken. Know anything about it? It sounds awesome." Ray talks fast, like he always does when he's nervous.

"I might've heard something." I nibble my lip.

"Listen, Lys." He sighs. "You rock and I suck." He takes a deep breath. "Keeping all distractions out of my life as I was told to just makes me more distracted. I should've called. Should've told you how I can't stand it when I don't hear your voice. Hell, even when my trainer yells at me, he doesn't do it half as well as you. You should probably give him some tips."

I laugh into the phone while a few tears stream down my cheeks.

"Bottom line. I need you, Lys. And not for the Kraken, or for the fight, but forever. I always needed you; it just took me a while to figure it out. I got a second chance in the ring but it means nothing if I don't get a second chance with you."

I close my eyes and breathe deep, quickly wiping the tears away from my eyes. "You never lost me." I lean back into the headrest of my car.

"Come to Vegas. I got a suite at the Venetian, a view of the strip, KISS blasting on the radio, and a first-class ticket waiting for you at the airport. I need you in my corner."

How can I say no? I need to tell him everything. About Jared, about Tommy, about the rigged fight, but right now there's only one thing he needs to hear. "I'm always in your corner."

"Gotta go, Jack, my trainer is about to break down my door. Flight leaves Thursday at 1 p.m. See ya soon."

He yells, "Jesus Christ, I'm coming," before hanging up the phone.

I drop my phone onto the seat and tap the steering wheel. An ear-to-ear smile graces my face. All the built-up tension releases from my body for a split second and a state of bliss takes over. And then…reality hits. Why does the most romantic phone call of my life have to happen around a web of chaos?

I check my email quick to make sure all my ducks are in a row at the Kraken. Wait a minute. If there's anywhere I can find concrete proof of sabotage, it's in Jared's email account. Doubt he even knows how to delete a message, and there's no way he'd actually organize anything. It's a miracle he can sign on. I click out of my Gmail account and sign into Jared's old AOL one. No way in hell he'd ever change his password. It's amazing he could remember Jared1017. If it wasn't his birthday he'd be locked out on a daily basis. I click on the mail icon.

A bunch of emails from RosieB94. Okay, the year I was born. If she's local that means we went to high school together. I flash through my yearbook in my mind no one stands out. Whatever, the most I can hope for is that he found someone else and he's moved on, just like me. I slide the curser to the message and click. Dear God, please don't let me see any body parts. I focus on the letters on the screen.

Jared,

I found this information in the chart. He's got severe damage to his left eye. Slight trauma can cause temporary blindness and a huge hit he can lose his sight for good or cause a bleed maybe even affecting his brain.

Hope this helps.

RJ

An atomic bomb goes off in my brain. RJ Baretta? You've got to be kidding me. She's the receptionist at Dr. Kline's office since her stripper career failed her. Heat rushes through my body. She broke a ton of laws. How could she be such a moron? Sending it to Jared in writing was the nail in her coffin and I'm the undertaker.

I hop up from my seat and take a screen shot of the email. Now I have proof. No need for Ray to take only my word, or the boxing commission for that matter. Tommy and Jared are going down.

I have to be there for Ray and I'm going to Vegas, but I

can't let him fight. It's an ambush and he has no idea. I'm the only one who can save him and now I've got a way to do it.

That's my plan and I'm sticking to it. I keep repeating the mantra over again in my mind. The fight is tomorrow night and I need to tell Ray everything as soon as we're face-to-face. Well…after we get reacquainted.

Dear God I wish I had more time. His trainer won't allow any significant others around until the day before the fight. Like a few more days is going to make such a difference.

My stomach turns. What am I thinking? I need to get Ray to bow out of this fight. Should I tell Jack, his trainer, what's going on? I sigh. No way, he'd probably give him some *Rocky* speech about overcoming adversity, or rising up. Hate to break it to him, but in real life things like that don't happen very often and most of the time you just get hurt.

Rick had a gift for spotting a scam a mile away and for waking Ray up to reality. When Ray won the Golden Gloves Championship he was the hero of the town. Right before he signed on with Dennis, Mr. Potter wanted to be his manager. Mr. Potter is a big-wig from Misty Harbor, the next town over. He pretty much owned every hotel in town. Well, clearly he saw Ray as his next business venture, and filled his mind with illusions of fortune and fame even though he didn't know a thing about boxing. Ray was caught up in fantasy land but Rick was there to pull him into reality.

Rick grabbed Ray by the shoulders and looked him straight in the eye. "Dude, this is bullshit."

Ray stared for a minute and then something flipped inside. "Jesus, you're right."

And that's all it took. Dear God, I hope I can have half as good as a result. No matter what I need to make him understand. I've got to find some way to throw him back into reality and stop this massacre.

I take a deep breath. The first step is getting there. I fling my over-packed suitcase into my trunk. Ready or not, here I come.

The seconds seem like hours. I glance at huge clock on the far wall of the terminal. Thirty more minutes till boarding. My foot shakes the whole row of chairs. It's probably moving faster than the propellers at this point. I nibble my nails. How the hell am I going to make it through this five-hour flight if I'm freaking out while waiting thirty minutes?

"Flight 135 to Las Vegas" blares over the loudspeaker.

I grab my purse and spring up from the seat.

"...has been delayed due to thunderstorms."

What? No way, this can't be happening. I run up to the podium.

"Excuse me, did you say the flight to Las Vegas is postponed?" I grip the strap of my purse.

"Yes ma'am, there are strong storms over the Midwest. The flight is cancelled until tomorrow at noon. We can offer you a hotel voucher."

All the blood drains from my face. No...I'll never make it in time.

"Are there any other flights? Any other airlines? I need to get to Vegas!" I scream so loud airport security takes a few steps towards me.

"Sorry, ma'am. All flights are postponed due to the weather. Noon tomorrow is the soonest flight to Las Vegas. We're very sorry for any inconvenience." The flight attendant smiles a fake smile that might as well be tattooed across her face.

I nod. "Thank you."

Causing a scene and getting detained by airport security won't make anything better for me. Ugh, why can't I beam myself over to Las Vegas like they do in *Star Trek*? Okay, calm down. Think, Lys. If the flight leaves at noon, you'll get there by five which is around 2 p.m. Pacific. There's still time to talk to Ray and get him to bow out. I can't give up, not now and not ever.

The vinyl chairs of the terminal grip me like a glove. I got here two hours early trying to avoid any other issues that might prevent me from getting to Las Vegas. I stare at the tele-prompters waiting for the status to change to Boarding.

Ugh, I've got to focus on something else or I'll go crazy before I get on the plane. I pull my cell phone from my purse and scroll through the texts from Ray.

Damn sandstorms. Guess we'll have to stay a few extra days once I win this fight. You're gonna love it here, Lys.

Okay, that just made me more stressed. Come on…I never asked for much. Right now I need divine intervention. Please

Fight for It

God, let me get to Vegas and stop this fight. I close my eyes and take a deep breath.

"Flight 135 to Las Vegas is delayed until 2 p.m." blares across the terminal.

My stomach drops to the floor. Why the hell is the universe against me? I spring from my seat and pace the length of the row of blue chairs. I'm at the mercy of the gods of time.

A vodka and cranberry, two *Star Wars* movies, and a chicken dinner on a tray later, we're about to land. Thank God the flight wasn't cancelled a third time. Maybe someone up there is on my side. I grip the strap of my purse, not out of fear of flying but so I can take off like a gazelle the second the door opens. The plane leans forward and a few minutes later, the wheels touch the ground.

Last time I flew was when we all went to Aruba for Mom and Dad's twenty-fifth anniversary. God, that was a whole world away. I was just as eager to get off of the plane then. Of course, Rick tried to tease me and block the gate. I'm confident I won't have to scream "I have to pee, this time in order to get through the crowd but I'll do whatever it takes.

The doors open and I leap into the aisle. The flight attendant's eyes widen and she moves to the side. I walk so fast I'm almost running. The second I'm in the terminal, I rip my cell phone out of my purse and dial Ray.

"Viva Las Vegas," he answers.

My heart races the second I hear his voice. "I'm here. I

need to talk to you." No time for the face-to-face I was hoping for, but he needs to know everything.

"Hey," Ray's voice is muted.

"Sweetheart, we're heading to the MGM now. Time to focus, I'm taking his phone," Jack, his trainer says.

"Wait!" I scream so loud about ten people walking by stare at me.

Jack hangs up.

I check the time. Oh my God, an hour to the fight. How the hell am I going to make it in time? Tears stream down my face. I swipe them away. Come on, Lys. Time to put on your big girl panties and make this happen. I rush toward the steps to take me down to the ground level to get a cab. The hell with my checked bag, I'll walk around naked if it saves Ray.

I rush through the automatic door. The hot air hits me as if I just walked into a sauna. I wave my arms like I'm about to land a plane.

A man walks over to me. "May I help you?"

His nametag says Rick. It's got to be a sign. "Yes, I need a cab. I'm in a hurry."

He gestures toward a line that says *Cabs*. Okay, so you don't need to hunt one down like you do in New York City. I stand in the line. Only two people ahead of me. For once, things are looking a bit better.

"Thank you," I say.

Five minutes later, I'm up. I open the back door of the cab and leap inside.

"Where to, ma'am?"

"MGM please." I rip out my wallet and hold it in my hand.

"Do you want to stop to take a picture by the Las Vegas sign or see any sights on the way?"

"Nope." The only sight I want to see is Ray telling everyone he's out and not going to fight. "I'm in a huge hurry."

He pulls out onto the road. I glance at my watch. Okay, forty minutes until fight time. It's cutting it really close but I still have some time. God, how the hell am I going to convince him to bow out this late in the game? At this point he can call me crazy or anything else in the book. I don't care. Right now, I'm in crazy mode.

We pull onto the road leading to the strip and it's bumper-to-bumper traffic. I lean my head out of the window, trying to see the hold up.

"Is it always this crowded?" It is a city with a ton of people. Maybe it's normal traffic.

"Nah. Probably an accident or something."

No. Not now. Are you freaking kidding me?

I glance at my phone. Thirty minutes until fight time. My knee bounces, shaking the seat of the cab. Ten minutes and we're barely on the strip.

The cab driver points ahead. "There's the MGM."

I gaze at a huge X-shaped building boasting the letters MGM Grand. It doesn't look that far. I can make it. "I'll walk from here. It will be quicker." I glance at the meter and hand him the money.

"Things are farther than they seem."

"I'll take my chances. Thanks." I hop out of the cab and onto the sidewalk.

Warm air engulfs me like I'm roasting in the oven. I take

off running and slithering through the crowd of people. Sweat droplets form on my hairline.

I look ahead to the huge sign which seems like it's getting further away rather than closer. Okay so the buildings look like they are closer than they are in reality. A mirage, common in the desert. Doesn't matter, it's my only chance.

I trek forward, the heat slowing me down a bit. Why do I feel like I'm walking through the fires of hell? I shake off the negative thoughts and keep going. I can't stop now. An eternity passes, which in reality is around ten minutes, and I see the glass doors at the entrance.

A burst of energy flows through me. I sprint toward the doors and rush inside. A blast of artic air hits me, shocking my body like a rush of adrenaline. I gaze around at the fortress I entered. Gold hues as far as the eye can see. Lights shining along the ceiling like stars. In the center of the floor stands a golden lion surrounded by an array of flowers in what looks like a fountain without the water. Dear God, it's like a palace. Nothing like this exists anywhere near Sunset Cove.

No time to admire the hotel. I've got to get to Ray. I jog toward the front desk.

"Hey...Ma'am," a voice yells.

A hand touches my shoulder. I stop and gaze at a man dressed in a black suit with a golden name tag sporting the letters *Josh Hotel Manager*. Oh no. My tickets. Wait they're in my carry-on. My heart beats a mile a minute. One more snag and I won't make it.

"I've got them right here." I dig in my bag and pull out the tickets. For once, I find what I'm looking for in my bag without searching forever.

He points toward the counter. "You need to check your bag at the front desk, for security reasons."

A roar erupts so loud I can hear it from the lobby. No way, I can't. "No time." I throw the bag at Josh and take off running.

I rush through the casino floor and swing a right, passing out Morimoto and stop at Blizz. *Welcome to the Jungle* blasts through the air.

Oh God, please don't let me be too late. My stomach drops to the floor. Come on Lys, you got this. I hold my tickets in the air and burst through the door.

An attendant grabs me and checks out my tickets with his flashlight. "Go." He points forward.

Finally, someone is actually helping me. I hop down the steps, trying not to pummel. I navigate the dark arena, only lit by flashes of light and the spotlight on the ring. The crowd cheers as Ray makes his way to the ring. I reach the bottom steps when I'm stopped by another attendant. He checks out my tickets and points to the front row.

Ray slides underneath the ropes and shadow boxes for the crowd. I shimmy through the people already in their seats and make my way to Ray's corner.

"Ray!" I yell. My voice is lost in an endless sea of noise. I race toward him, flailing my hands in the air.

He moves his neck from side-to-side, probably stretching his muscles, and catches a glimpse of me. He stops and points his glove in my direction.

A weight lifts from my shoulders. A guy from his training team comes over to me and escorts me to his corner. I struggle to make it to Ray. It's like I've already gone twelve rounds with

Mike Tyson. I rush toward Ray, wrapping my arms around him.

"Your entrance might be better than mine. You made it, Lys." He kisses my forehead.

"Ray, you can't fight," I mutter in between trying to catch my breath.

He scrunches his eyebrows. "It's a little late for that, Lys." He presses his forehead against mine. "Don't worry. It'll be over soon. I'm ready."

I shake my head. "You can't... It's a set-up."

"What are you talking about?" He stands up. "Don't let nerves get the best of you. I never do."

"Ray, listen to me. Tommy is Jared's cousin. He knows all about your injury. R.J. from the doctor's office told him all about your eye. He's going to try to take you out...for good. You've got to call this off."

"Alright, that's enough." Jack, Ray's trainer, wraps his arms around me and pulls me out of the ring. He carries me to my seat and runs back to the ring. "You'll get massacred if your head isn't in this fight. She's just scared. Shake it off and focus."

I bow my head in defeat. Tears stream down my face.

Thunderstruck by AC/DC blasts through the air as Tommy makes his way to the ring. His entourage treks behind him. They march down the aisle, Tommy holding his arm in the air like he's doing a fist pump. The crowd goes wild. Tommy makes his way to the ring and points his glove at Ray. Ray mocks his move.

I nibble my nails. Ray stares at me, his eyes looking to the depths of my soul. I'd never hurt him or try to sabotage his comeback. He knows me better than anyone. All I want is to spend forever with him and I want forever to last more than twelve rounds.

I can't sit here and give up. I have to do something… anything. The crowd lulls as the announcer makes his way to the ring.

I jump up from my seat and make a megaphone with my hands. "Dude, this is bullshit." The words flow out of my mouth like someone else was speaking them.

Ray's eyes widen. He turns toward his trainer and shakes his head, waving his hands in an X motion.

His trainer, Jack, throws in hands in the air. He screams so many obscenities at Ray so fast his words aren't even coherent.

Ray calls for the referee. The announcer leaves the ring and the referee takes his place. Ray walks toward him and Tommy follows suit so they're staring each other down with the referee in between them.

The crowd hoots and hollers, breaking out into cheers as if it's all part of the show. My heart pounds and adrenaline flows through my veins at warp speed. I grip my hands together tight.

The referee talks to Ray and then to relays the information to Tommy. Please God let this all be over. Tommy throws his hands in the air and pushes the referee. The ref falls, sliding across the ring. Oh my God, Tommy's lost it. An array of security personnel come to the aid of the ref.

I cover my mouth with my hands. Memories of Jared flipping out flood my mind. The temperament must run in the family. I stand frozen.

Tommy's face turns pure red. He screams at Ray, spittle

building in the corner of his mouth. Ray screams back. None of their words are audible over the roaring crowd, but I know what's going down. Tommy turns for a spit second, as if he's walking back to his corner, but then pivots. He rushes toward Ray like a freight train and cold cocks him smack in the left eye. Ray covers his face with his arms and drops to the floor.

Security rushes to the ring like they're the Secret Service. I drop my hands and rush toward the ring, trying to push through the mound of people. It's no use. I sway my head from side-to-side to get a glimpse of Ray. Dear God, please let him be alright.

A security person waves his arms toward the medical staff, bringing a stretcher toward the ring. My stomach drops to the floor. Within minutes, Ray is whisked out of the arena and Tommy is subdued by at least a dozen security guards. I stand helpless, alone in a sea of people.

"I always had a thing for pirates." I hop onto the barstool next to Ray.

"Argh. Shiver me timbers." Ray adjusts the strap of his eye patch.

A month and two surgeries later, Ray is finally back at the Kraken. Thank God there was only damage to the optic nerve and no brain bleeds. Dr. Kline thinks he'll be able to see as well as he did before once the nerve damage heals. And now he has officially retired from fighting…for good.

The National Boxing Association pulled Tommy's boxing license. Guess he'll have to join the ranks of the rest of the world after his fit of rage at the fight. R.J. lost her job at Dr. Kline's office for violating the federal patient privacy act. Ray's lawyers are having a field day filing law suits against the two of them. Of course, Jared lurks in the shadows, but everyone knows exactly what he did. His family name is tarnished beyond repair.

I glance over at the dance floor on the deck. The whole town watched the fight go down here on Pay-Per-View and ever since the Kraken has been the most hopping place in town. Just like Ray pictured it.

Beth by KISS blasts through the air. I customized a few songs in the juke box to add a bit of nostalgia.

Ray raises an eyebrow and comes out from behind the bar. He walks over to me and holds out his hand. "Wanna dance?"

Hell, yes. I've wanted to dance with him on the deck of the Kraken since I was a sophomore in high school. "Sure."

He takes my hand and we walk onto the dance floor. He pulls me close and we sway together in unison. The aroma of his Woodland Creek cologne flows through the air, taking me back to our glory days.

"You know what's crazy?" he says.

Pretty much the last few months of my life. "Dazzle me."

He smiles. "One of the things I miss about boxing is the interview right after the fight in the ring."

"You mean when Rocky screams 'Adrian…I did it.'"

He nods. "Yeah. You're all beat-up and exhausted but that moment…you shine."

I scrunch my eyebrows. "Well, since your fighting days are over I guess we'll have to conduct that interview right now."

"It's a little late for that."

"It's never too late." I stop and take a step back from him. I clench my right hand into my best microphone shape. I hold it up to my mouth. "So Ray, this was your last fight. What have you gotten out of it?" I hold my hand toward his mouth.

He stops for a minute, like he's in deep thought and then smiles. He pulls me close, pressing his forehead against mine. "I won it all. I got the girl."

The End.

ABOUT THE AUTHOR

USA Today Bestselling author Amy L Gale is a romance author by night, pharmacist by day, who loves rock music and the feel of sand between her toes. She's the author of USA Today Bestsellers *Resisting Darkness* and *Resisting Moonlight;* Amazon New Adult Bestsellers, *Blissful Tragedy and Blissful Valentine,* along with *Christmas Blitz,* and *Blissful Disaster, Bear Creek Cowboys: Bear Creek Rodeo series, Mine Before Midnight,* and *Pull Me Under.* When she's not writing, she enjoys baking, scary movies, rock concerts, and reading books at the beach. She lives in the lush forest of northeastern Pennsylvania with her husband, daughter, seven cats, and golden retriever, Sadie. You can find her at www.authoramygale.com, www.twitter.com/amyg618, https://www.facebook.com/pages/Amy-Gale/540928695977160

Read More from Amy L. Gale
www.authoramygale.com

Made in the USA
Middletown, DE
22 July 2025